Books by
MARGERY SHARP

The Lost
Chapel
Picnic

The Lost Chapel Picnic

and Other Stories

MARGERY SHARP

Little, Brown and Company · Boston · Toronto

FIRST AMERICAN EDITION

TO 7/73

The author is grateful to Liberty Library Corporation for permission to reprint the story, "Mr Hamble's Bear," originally published under the title "Very Much Alive." Copyright 1942 by Macfadden Publications, Inc.

Library of Congress Cataloging in Publication Data

Sharp, Margery, 1905-
    The lost chapel picnic, and other stories.

    CONTENTS: Lost chapel picnic.--Mr. Hamble's bear.--
George Lambert and Miss P.--[Etc.]
    I. Title.
PZ3.S5316Lo [PR6037.H334]   823'.9'12   73-6733
ISBN 0-316-782939

PRINTED IN THE UNITED STATES OF AMERICA

Contents

The Lost
Chapel
Picnic

The Lost Chapel Picnic

FACED WITH SO enormous and complex a subject as the Lost Chapel Picnic (six miles each way, on bicycles), one hardly knows where to start. To any member of the Bly family it is like starting to write about the French Revolution, or the United States of America – there is so much to bring in. Nor can one safely generalize; even the statement that it took place every summer, for instance, at once calls to mind the summers when it didn't, such as 1927 (chicken-pox) and 1940 (Battle of Britain). Only its essential characteristic was constant: the Lost Chapel picnic always took place in rain.

Even for England, it was remarkable. Lost Chapels – an abbreviation also employed in such constructions as 'to go on a Lost Chapel', or 'to go Lost Chapelling' – happened invariably, and only, in August, when we children were home from school and friends stayed holidaying round about; but however brilliant the weather before and after, it always rained for Lost Chapel. In time this became so notorious that ladies planning garden-parties, or Vicars organizing fêtes, used to enquire of my Aunt in advance what date had been fixed, to avoid it. Theoretically, of course, it should have been possible to wait for a really fine afternoon, fling together sufficient provisions, and set off *à l'improviste*. But that wouldn't have suited us Blys at all. A Lost Chapel was not only a serious event, to be looked forward to for at least ten days, but also, so to speak, a serious *sporting* event, which we would have scorned to rig. Moreover, one of its most important and beloved features, the pony-cart, had to be hired ahead of time. No one rode in the cart, but we needed it to carry enough kindling and firewood to build a good big fire. The fire was to dry ourselves at, because it always rained; and if there was a sort of circular lunacy about the whole scheme, no Bly ever seemed to notice. Getting first wet through and then rough dried, was what one *did*, on a Lost Chapel.

Who first found the Lost Chapel, my cousin Bryan or my cousin Sarah?

Bryan's juvenile claim was that he actually lived there, for several months, when at the age of six he left home to become a bandit. No one took this seriously, since he was well known to have been back in time for tea. If he saw the Lost Chapel at all, he didn't mention it at the time. Sarah, rather cleverly, was completely vague; she said she'd just found Lost Chapel one day when she was out by herself, and thought she'd told everyone, though she mightn't have. This point remains mysterious. In any case, by about 1924 we were going there regularly.

No one knew either who first gave the place its name. It almost certainly wasn't a chapel at all, but the barn of a pulled-down farm. Nor was it lost, in the sense of being hidden or unknown: it could be seen, high up on a spur of moorland, from any point in our village. It was still remote. Of the six miles we had to cover to reach it, only three lay along a proper road; at the third milestone one had to turn through a gap and pedal desperately up a narrow slippery track. (From this point the pony was led). Here heather grew on either hand, thinning as one ascended, then thinning out again to what was called the tundra-line – beyond which there was only grass again much shorter and less lush than the grass below. (When the sun shone it must have been very hot up there. But we went to

2

Lost Chapel only for the picnic, only once a year. It was one of those rules children make for themselves in their perennial quest for stability). Then the last fifty yards or so flattened out, and there the farm and its buildings must once have stood. Now only the barn was left, big and high, stone-floored, and very dark inside ...

Solemnly dark; the first few moments, before we lit the fire and set up the oil-stove, were always rather hushed. We children would fling down our bicycles and race in, panting and noisy, sweating under our wet mackintoshes – and for a moment be hushed. It was the moment, in a way, we came for; we always tried to arrive before the adults. (Actually this was easy, the last half-mile on grass winded them so). For a moment we would all stand silent, by ourselves, savouring the solemn dark; perhaps it was in the first of such moments that we gave the place its name. It was just *like* a chapel. As a matter of fact, my cousin Alan Bly got married in it. He didn't tell me this till many years afterwards, but at the 1926 picnic, while the rest of us were cooking sausages, he took a little girl called Sybil Addis aside, proposed, was accepted, and immediately twisted a paper-clip round her finger, announcing 'With this paper-clip I thee wed.' He was then twelve, and Sybil ten; he had been immensely struck both by her curly red hair and her uphill cycling, and felt she shouldn't be missed. His instinct was absolutely sound: they were re-married in '38, on which occasion I stood bridesmaid.

But to leap to such an episode, in the history of Lost Chapels, is like leaping to the execution of Marie Antoinette in the history of the French Revolution, or to the Boston Tea-Party in the history of the United States ...

The nucleus of all Lost Chapels – the Pilgrim Fathers, so to speak – consisted of my Aunt Mary and Uncle James, my cousins Alan, Bryan and Sarah, and myself. The friends we children invited varied from year to year, especially as we grew older, but numbered usually five or six. There were also several adults, known as Steadies, who had somehow got involved.

The leading Steady was Miss Pargiter, an elderly spinster who spent most of the year in Italy, but whose hardy frame had successfully resisted all Capuan blandishments: one of our best cyclists on the flat, and very game up-hill.

Mr Adrian, also elderly, there was some slight mystery about. The village believed he'd been in jail. Whether or not this was true – and he certainly led a very solitary life, painting water-colours in a cottage like a picture-postcard – my Aunt had long decided there was no harm in him. Mr Adrian loved Lost Chapels because they were the only things he was ever invited to, and did the view from the hill each year. (Another reason why we had to have the pony-cart: to tote Mr Adrian's easel. He was a water-colourist of the old school, with an immense amount of baggage).

The third Steady was comparatively young – kind Mr Gore-Willoughby, for eleven months of the year a London stock-broker, whose ridiculous name we children used to chant in unison as he toiled up the last lap. Someone, I forget who, said he Lost Chapelled simply to get his weight down, but this was a lie, because he always brought, and partook of, a large box of marrons glacés. They were the only marrons we ever set tooth to, but we liked him for himself as well, in a rather offhand, patronizing way, and his bicycle had a three-speed gear.

All participants wore their oldest clothes, under mackintoshes.

It was considered legitimate in an adult to dismount for the last lap, but absolutely no one was let ride in the pony-cart.

And no one, however wet or tired, could expect sympathy if they grizzled.

Here we come to something really important about Lost Chapels. (The Tennis-Court Oath, the Declaration of Independence). As we children grew up, they provided a wonderful testing-ground for the current objects of our affections. Alan, as has been related, grasped this point extremely early; but his brother Bryan between '31 and '36 tried out at least five possibles. They all, with the exception of Milly Blanchard, started fairly level: nice, pretty girls every one, all of course with bicycles, and all with an abundance of good-will. My cousin Bryan was an extremely taking youth. Milly Blanchard was nice only technically – as it were in the eyes of a jury of matrons. Her father was our chemist, and so quite hopelessly in trade. Only one damsel, as I remember, failed to complete the course, but two were literally washed out at the post. They looked, said Bryan disgustedly, *wet*. Of course they *were* wet, poor creatures, but we all knew what he meant. The fourth entry failed on sensibility. We Blys never thought of ourselves as in the least artistic, in fact we rather derided Art – poor Mr Adrian's hobby. It never occurred to us that one reason we so loved Lost Chapel was for its romantic beauty. But when Cecilia White called it *pokey*, every Bly hackle rose. So Milly Blanchard was left with a clear field. She was full of running anyway. She hadn't even a permanent wave, but she braided her long wet hair like a Red Indian's, and wrapped herself in a rug, and did a war-dance all round the oil-stove. She was undeniably rowdy. She also, in due course, made my cousin Bryan an excellent wife.

The most exciting thing that ever happened on a Lost Chapel was when the oil-stove caught fire. No one ever discovered the cause; simply all at once, in an instant, blue and yellow flames were running swiftly across the flag-stones *after Miss Pargiter*. It was this that made the excitement: we were all tough, experienced Lost Chapellers, perfectly capable of estimating the comparative slightness of the danger – the floor, as has been said, was stone, all we had to do was stand clear until the oil burnt itself out. But they ran, the little blue flames, *after* Miss Pargiter – one really couldn't believe without a conscious sense of fun. Because Miss Pargiter, instead of making sensibly for the door, skipped back and back directly in their path. 'Sideways, you Juggins!' shouted my cousin Alan. 'Jump sideways, and let 'em go by!' This was the first time any one of us children had ever shouted at an adult, and Alan wasn't even made to apologize. The episode opened new vistas all round – as my Aunt subsequently lamented; but some fifteen years later I myself most profitably shouted, 'Down, you Juggins!' at a full General caught beside me in the street during a London blitz.

The most scandalous thing that ever happened was the snatching of a quite personable millionaire by the Vicarage Kids' new governess. An episode (1930) not strictly Bly, but Bly by repercussion.

He was staying, Mr Richards, at the local inn: to cast a casual, millionairish eye over the inn itself, and a couple of farms, which he'd been left (in the way millionaires do get left such trifles), by a comparatively poor relation. My Aunt invited him to Lost Chapel out of pure kind-heartedness, because she thought he looked lonely. Sarah and I were both still in the schoolroom – as I dare say Mr Richards knew, at fifty he was still unmarried, which shows how knowing he'd been for years. It was also out of sheer kind-heartedness that my Aunt invited Miss Dove. I remember how all we children protested, saying she'd never get up the hill. We disliked Miss Dove, which in a way was odd, since we also disliked the Vicarage Kids; as a rule any governess who gave them hell had our enthusiastic support. But in fact everyone rather disliked Miss Dove. Though of English parentage she had been born and reared in Paris; which of course gave her a wonderful French accent, but also, in some mysterious way, enabled her to dress quite unsuitably well. She turned up for Lost Chapel in beautifully cut tweeds, also a small felt hat with a pheasant's wing. My Aunt and Miss Pargiter wore sou'westers, tied firmly under the chin. Even Cecilia White had worn a skiing cap. 'Haven't you a mackintosh, Miss Dove?' enquired my Aunt solicitously. 'It's almost certain to rain? And won't your pretty hat be quite spoiled?' Miss Dove said smilingly that she would risk it.

The rest of the party as usual looked like a bunch of tramps. I remember that Mr Adrian had had the brilliant idea of putting his head in a sponge-bag. He was undeniably a little odd. But wait! – his hour is yet to come.

Miss Dove, as she gracefully mounted her bicycle, cut an extremely elegant figure; and all we children cheered up at the thought of seeing her drenched.

Mr Richards my Aunt provided with the bicycle of our garden-boy. I think he found the whole affair pretty surprising: he didn't know about Lost Chapels, and I dare say had anticipated some far milder excursion. When he realized the awful truth, he in fact at once suggested using his Rolls. But after we explained how soon the proper road ended, he resigned himself – all too literally – to his fate. For exactly at the proper road's end, though it was hardly raining at all, Miss Dove dismounted from her bicycle and *stopped*.

We could hardly believe it. No one ever *stopped*, on a Lost Chapel. 'A little *riposo*?' called Miss Pargiter, pedalling gamely by. 'Don't think it's going to clear!' warned Uncle James cheerily. 'Best foot forwards, Miss Dove, best foot forward!' 'I'm going home,' replied Miss Dove, calmly propping her machine against the hedge. 'Come, come, come, come, come!' piped Mr Adrian – flat over his handlebars. Cool as a cucumber, and with a brazenness to take the breath, Miss Dove neatly cut out Mr Richards from the tail of our convoy and asked him to cycle back and get his car, and take her home.

Nothing succeeds like audacity – especially if one is practically a Frenchwoman. Mr Richards, offered this splendid excuse for abandoning the whole project, at once reversed direction. We heard later that they spent the rest of the day driving about in his Rolls, inspecting his various properties, also taking tea at an hotel. Miss Dove had about four hours clear run, and at the end of it killed. For if Mr Richards didn't actually propose that afternoon, or if what he did propose wasn't actually marriage, Miss Dove undoubtedly quitted the village at the same time as he did – rightly confident, as it proved, of bringing him to the legal point in due course.

The Bly aspect of this was that during Mr Richards' call of apology, to say how sorry he'd been to miss Lost Chapel, the conversation somehow turned to the shipping industry, in which Mr Richards had large interests, and in which my Cousin Alan now does so well.

Perhaps there was a repercussion on my Cousin Sarah also. If I have as yet barely mentioned Sarah, it is because she was in general so self-effacing. Her clever claim to the discovery of Lost Chapel is remembered for its unusualness – as a rule she didn't claim so much as a pet rabbit, just let each litter be divided among the rest of us, and fed them when we forgot. She was the perfect elder sister, elder cousin; her kind plain face perfectly reflected, except in beauty, a disposition very nearly angelic. But she really was plain, and when in 1934 a new young doctor came to flutter every female heart, we Blys frankly regretted that Sarah hadn't a hope. Because we all liked Dr Henderson at once, and would have welcomed him into the family – whereas if Sarah went on not getting engaged, and she was then twenty-one, we feared she might well end up with the curate.

Dr Henderson Lost Chapelled and liked it. (One of the reasons why we approved of him). He came *again*. ('34, '35 and '36). And at the '36 Lost Chapel my Cousin Sarah, possibly remembering how well audacity had succeeded with Miss Dove, quietly and self-effacingly proposed to him.

If self-effacingness and audacity hardly chime together, let us say that Sarah performed the audacious deed as self-effacingly as possible.

The rest of us were all gathered round the fire. It was one of the wettest Lost Chapels I remember. But even dripping, Dr Henderson still looked wonderfully handsome. Sarah looked her plainest; but at least, so to speak, *indestructible*. With her mouse-brown hair pushed damply back from her forehead, without a trace of make-up on a face just scrubbed dry – there Sarah stood, take her or leave her, and suddenly asked Dr Henderson to come outside. It was pouring cats and dogs. Rain drove into the turf, if the turf hadn't been so sodden the rain would have bounced off. But out Dr Henderson went. And out in the rain, keeping her gaze firmly fixed on the storm-swept valley below, Sarah said, 'I love you with all my heart. I think I would make a very good doctor's wife. If you'll never want to marry me, will you please say so now, so I can go into a convent and be a nun.'

No doubt it was a very different approach from Miss Dove's. It happened to be just what Dr Henderson would have ordered

9

for himself. (He often told us afterwards how bedevilled he'd been by too many attractive patients.) Of course neither Alan nor Bryan nor I thought of eavesdropping, we were most honourably *not* eavesdropping; what Sarah said she told me herself in case it might ever be useful to me. But we were somewhere near the door, and we did happen to see Dr Henderson suddenly take Sarah's hand, and hear him call her 'My splendid honest girl. . . .'

They came in again almost at once. They had to, because it started to hail as well, and Mr Adrian ran out with his umbrella. And Sarah cooked Dr Henderson's sausages very carefully, and he tried to make her eat them, and that has been the pattern of their lives ever since.

Mr Adrian's hour of glory. This struck some time in the 'thirties, when he astonishingly induced a small London gallery to exhibit a batch of his water-colours. They were all of the same view, in rain. (Naturally; all executed on Lost Chapels.) More astonishing still, he won a small but definite *succès d'estime*: the novelty of such monotony, as it were, struck several critics to admiration, and four of his wettest gems actually found purchasers. As a result Mr Adrian's social life quite bloomed, and besides going on Lost Chapels he went out to tea right and left. He didn't, however, as we half expected, lay his heart and press-cuttings at the feet of Miss Pargiter; they remained individual Steadies to the end.

Kind Mr Gore-Willoughby I married myself; to my immense surprise, he turned out to be no more than twelve years my senior. And we too plighted our troth, like Alan and Sybil, and Bryan and Milly and Sarah and Dr Henderson, on a Lost Chapel – I apparently looking like a mermaid, and he without doubt resembling a seal. For of course it was pouring cats and dogs as usual, because Lost Chapels always took place in rain. . . .

They still do. We still take the pony-cart (though with a new pony), to carry sufficient firewood and kindling to build a good big fire. Mr Adrian and Miss Pargiter no longer pedal gamely beside us, nor my kind uncle and aunt; we have acquired several fresh Steadies, however, and of course there are the children. Alan's three boys come, and Sarah's boy and girl, Bryan's two daughters, my own twins and their elder sister.

Obviously the subject is too vast. There is too much to bring in. It's like writing the history of the French Revolution, or of the United States – writing about our Lost Chapel picnics, six miles, (by bicycle), each way.

Mr Hamble's Bear

SHERRARD had forty-five minutes to wait for his train, so as the day was fine he checked his suitcase and turned out into the Euston Road. He had three days' leave from his wartime work at the Admiralty, and was about to spend two of them in unpleasant travel in order to keep a luncheon engagement in Scotland.

As he strolled along, finding the minutes pass slowly and the wind colder than he had thought, the sight of a tobacconist's reminded him that he was short of cigarettes. The tiny shop did not look as though it stocked his rather expensive brand, but pausing outside it he was struck by the oddity of the window. The boxes and packets, the dummies and display-cards, showed no attempt at arrangement: they were simply piled in one corner, leaving the rest of the space bare. The original legend on the fascia had been smudged out with what looked like tar, and the name 'Hamble' roughly substituted. The whole establishment, in fact, had a take-it-or-leave-it air which Sherrard found unusual. He liked the unusual. He went in.

Behind the counter sat a large unshaven old man wearing a knotted handkerchief instead of a collar. His jacket needed cleaning, or perhaps burning. His features were heavy and sad. But he had the aura of one who is his own master, and Sherrard rightly guessed him to be Hamble in person.

'Balkan 333?' enquired Sherrard.

'No,' said Mr Hamble.

'Well, what have you got?' asked Sherrard.

'Nothing much,' said Mr Hamble.

Sherrard looked round and saw that this was true. Even for wartime, the place was very poorly stocked. But there was a case of cigarette-holders, and as the lady he was going to visit lost about one a day, Sherrard began making a selection. To do so he put down on the counter a couple of books he had in his hand: a Euripides, in the original Greek, and a work on philosophy. They seemed to arouse Mr Hamble's interest. He looked at them, he picked them up, he flipped open the covers, noted the prices, studied the title-pages; then set them down again and considered Sherrard with new attention.

'You seem,' said Mr Hamble, 'to be a person of education.'

He spoke with a peculiar measured cadence, like a man unaccustomed to much talk, unaccustomed particularly to the give-and-take of conversation. The remark being a rather difficult one to answer, Sherrard merely nodded.

'And also,' pursued Mr Hamble, looking at Sherrard's suit, 'a man of the world.'

'I've seen a good deal of it,' said Sherrard.

Mr Hamble examined him thoughtfully for some minutes, and appeared to come to a decision.

'Do you mind,' he asked, 'if I tell you a rather remarkable story?'

Sherrard said not at all, he would be delighted.

'It's an animal story,' said Mr Hamble apologetically.

Sherrard said he would still be very glad to hear it. Mr Hamble settled himself comfortably against the counter, and cleared his throat. 'As a small child' (began Mr Hamble), 'I frequently spent my holidays with a maiden aunt who lived in a villa on the Italian Riviera. One day, as I was running back through the garden in response to the luncheon bell, I was surprised to see in my path a bear. Bears, in the imagination at least, are by no means unfamiliar objects to a small boy, and I daresay I should have taken it quite calmly but for the fact that it walked upon its hind legs, and also wore a small Homberg hat. I fled, howling. In but a few moments, of course, all was explained: the animal belonged to a band of gypsies who were exhibiting it through the neighbourhood, and hoped to offer us a private show. In this they were disappointed, my aunt being a strong supporter of the Royal Society for the Prevention of Cruelty to Animals. Her reactions were vigorous but inconsistent: she at once gave the bear-leader a lira to let the animal down on all fours, threatened to report him to the police, and sent the whole party round to the kitchen for scraps. Later that afternoon, in a secluded grove, I came upon them again, enjoying her bounty, in which the bear had his part. He was eating a cold leg of pigeon, and to do so had thrust back his furry muzzle, revealing a physiogomy very like that of his master (or accomplice).

'This incident made a deep impression on me, and for many years after I was a good deal confused in my relations with all the larger quadrupeds. At home in London, when taken to the Zoo, I was quite convinced that all lions and tigers, apes (and of course bears) were really human persons exercising a profession as regular as that of butcher or baker. This theory was strengthened by our annual visit to the pantomime, where Puss in Boots, or Red Riding Hood's Wolf, always doffed their masks to share in the final applause. Gradually, of course, the misapprehension was dispersed, and I was able to laugh with my parents at my earlier fancies. But I tell you all this so that you may understand why I have always been particularly attentive to, and perhaps easily influenced by, the personalities of animals.'

Sherrard said he understood perfectly.

'Years passed,' continued Mr Hamble. 'My parents died, leaving me but ill provided for. I had never been clever, but I found myself a niche in the second-hand furniture trade. My aunt also passed on, and from her I received a sum sufficient to set up a small business of my own in Praed Street, Paddington. My first independent purchase was a stuffed bear.'

He paused, evidently awaiting comment. Sherrard said he thought it very natural.

'It was *not* natural,' corrected Mr Hamble. 'The market for stuffed bears – upright – is extremely restricted. I did not intend bidding for it. My lips moved as it were of their own accord. 'Five pounds!' I cried; and the animal was mine.

'It cost another ten shillings in transport. I set it up on the pavement outside my shop, hoping to gain some advantage in the way of publicity. I placed a small Homberg hat on its head. It attracted, as I had hoped, considerable attention. Business looked up, and I rapidly disposed of a set of croquet mallets, a Windsor chair, and a steel engraving of the Empress Josephine.

'For the first week my new acquisition remained, so to speak, passive. Then one particularly sunny day I noticed that the Homberg hat looked very shabby, and I replaced it by a hard straw. Several passers-by noted the change with approval. The weather broke, it rained every day, and I grew very tired of either hauling the bear inside or wrapping him in dust sheets. I remembered a mackintosh cape, Inverness style, which had belonged to my father, and put that on him instead. You would have been surprised to see what a change it made. He still looked most like a bear, but he also looked rather like a German professor. My charwoman reported that he had given her quite a turn, and I noticed one or two customers murmur a word of apology as they brushed by. Perhaps the most curious point was that when the rainy spell ended, and I took the cape off, the bear looked not more, but less, natural. He looked unclad – like a German professor in his combinations. Fortunately, amongst a variety of second-hand clothes, I possessed an academic gown, which fitted him very well. I did not know what faculty it belonged to, but as I did not know either what the bear was professor of, this hardly mattered. At any rate, he was again decent.

'I ought to mention that he was already, in a small way, a public figure. Everyone in Paddington knew him, and the variety of his hats (for he had several others besides those I have mentioned) were a constant source of friendly interest; but this gown, by attracting the notice of the students of London University, opened wider spheres. I had observed for some time the presence of a new type of customer – young men in flannel trousers, tweed jackets, and large mufflers – who bought, if they bought anything, second-hand books: at last two of them approached me with an offer of five shillings for the loan of the bear for Saturday afternoon. They wished, they said, to take him to a football match. I thought it over; the bear had certainly done his best, he had brought me innumerable fresh customers, and it seemed hard that he should never have any pleasure. I decided to let him go – refusing, however, the five shillings. His new friends were delighted, and off he went in their car, wearing a large purple muffler and a knot of purple ribbon. I put in an umbrella after him, in case of rain.'

Mr Hamble paused.

'Perhaps,' he enquired, 'you know something of the ways of students?'

'I've been one myself,' said Sherrard.

'You surprise me,' said Mr Hamble. 'Though no doubt some of them turn out well. However, I knew nothing of them then, though I afterwards learnt a good deal. If I *had* known, I daresay I should not have been so amenable.'

'I hope he got back all right?' said Sherrard.

'He got *back*. He got back well after midnight, smelling strongly of drink, with his gown torn, and having lost his umbrella. I was extremely annoyed, and I spoke pretty sharply to his companions; but they were in no state to appreciate the justice of my remarks. In fact I doubt whether they heard them, for a day or two later they returned, quite unabashed, with an invitation to a Club dinner. This time I was harder to persuade, but they assured me it was to be a most decorous function, sanctioned by the University Authorities, and that the Club was one for the advancement of Theological Philosophy. I have mentioned already that the bear strongly resembled a German professor, and this seemed just the sort of thing he would enjoy. I let him accept. But I stipulated that I should call for him myself, at ten-thirty, and I actually did so, though I had some difficulty – the debate was still in full swing, and he was taking the chair – in getting him away.

'This incident too had consequences. The taxi fare was six-and-six – to me a not unimportant sum. In fact, I considered it far too much, and I very nearly decided he should not go out again. Then it occurred to me that it was really he who had sold the croquet-mallets, the Windsor chair, and the steel engraving of the Empress Josephine, at a profit of fifteen shillings; he was therefore entitled to at least that sum. Next day I began a separate account for him – on one side his personal sales, on the other taxi-fares, new clothes and so on. I counted as his all sales made to customers who looked at the bear before they looked in the window; and he did so well that he was soon able to buy himself an opera hat, a silk muffler, and a new umbrella – all very necessary, for from this time his engagements rapidly increased. Were you in London in '38?'

Sherrard said no, he had been abroad.

'Then you can have no idea,' said Mr Hamble impressively, 'how very popular he became. Perhaps it will help if I tell you that on certain occasions – Boat Race night, and the Cup Final – he had to have a special policeman detailed to look after him. Like a Cabinet Minister. He was the acknowledged patron of London University, without whom no academic function (of the lighter sort) was complete. He attended every sporting event, and usually finished the evening with the victorious team. He became a familiar figure on the news-films. He was several times kidnapped by medical students, for the medicals (always a turbulent element) wished to appropriate him entirely, and this led to a standing feud between the Colleges and the Hospitals. Each side wished to adopt him outright, but against this I set my face. I did not wish him to degenerate into a mere rowdy.

'My own life, of course, became more and more bound up with his, for I kept to my rule of always calling for him, and this rather cut me off from the social enjoyments of my neighbours, who were nearly all whist-players, and who disliked my having to leave in the middle of a hand. Soon I ceased to frequent them, and without regret. Tradesmen's card-parties had small charm for me; I breathed, vicariously, a wider air. I did once suffer a slight disappointment. A Miss Armiger, a lady friend in the clothing branch, one day came in with a couple of passes for the theatre, and asked me to be her escort. I looked at the date; it was impossible. We were engaged two deep – I had to call for the bear at nine, after a dinner at University

College, and take him on to a smoking concert at Guy's Hospital, and fetch him again at half-past ten. I refused Miss Armiger's invitation with deep regret, and while I was still explaining the circumstances, she left the shop.

'But let me,' said Mr Hamble, 'abridge. For a time all went well. Business continued to prosper. I did not perhaps keep our accounts as carefully as at first, and the bear was a bit extravagant, but I took pride in his appearance, and my own wants were few. The change in our relations came about very gradually. I began to feel a slight reluctance to turn out so frequently and so late at night. It annoyed me to hear people refer to the establishment as "The Bear's" instead of "Hamble's"; and one evening in November – the fifth – as I sat waiting to go and fetch him from a Guy Fawkes Dinner, these dissatisfactions came to a head. I had had a hard day's work, the fire burned brightly, there was a programme on the wireless I should have liked to hear. But at ten-fifteen out I would have to go. For the third time that week. It suddenly came over me that the people who called my shop "The Bear's" were right: it wasn't my shop at all, it was his. I was working twelve hours a day to support him in a life of idle pleasure. He still pulled his weight, in a sense; but of his many friends fewer and fewer made any substantial purchase. I got out my books: in the last two weeks he had sold only a couple of sixpenny novels, and his taxi fares alone amounted to thirty shillings.

'And there were other points – trifling, perhaps, that rankled. He was always losing umbrellas. It seemed absolutely impossible for him to go out with an umbrella and bring it back. And he lost not only his own, but mine as well, whenever I lent them him. And as I sat thinking over these things, and feeling how hard it was that in a few minutes I should have to leave my fire and go out, I suddenly came to an astounding decision.

19

'"All right," I said, "you can get back by yourself"; and I locked up and went to bed.'

Mr Hamble turned to Sherrard beseechingly.

'I assure you,' he said, 'I assure you, I never thought of anything more than his spending the night on the pavement, and having lost his umbrella and it coming on to rain. That was the very worst I anticipated. And in the morning – for it *did* rain – I hurried down at half-past six with a large towel. But he wasn't there. He hadn't come home. I waited till nine, and then I hurried to the College where he had dined. It was built round a quadrangle, in the centre of which, as I entered, I observed the remains of a large bonfire. I observed them quite idly. At the lodge I made enquiry of the porter, giving the names of the bear's particular hosts; only to be told that they were one and all in the hands of the police. They had gone, explained the porter, too far: a bonfire in the quad might pass, but not the carrying of flaming torches through the London streets. They had all been arrested. "Was there a bear arrested with them?" I asked. The porter shook his head; I felt a foolish relief. At least they had had the decency, I thought, not to implicate him. "Then, where is he?" I asked. "I have come to take him home". The porter shook his head again – but this time pityingly: and he pointed through the lodge-window to the heap of ash . . .'

'What!' cried Sherrard, genuinely shocked. 'He'd been burnt?'

'Cremated. I knew without another word. I asked, "What time did they light it?" – and the porter answered, "About half-past ten".'

There is always something a little absurd in the emotions of the stout. Mr Hamble was very stout indeed, and the object of his affection a stuffed bear; yet Sherrard did not find his distresss wholly ridiculous. It was too sincere. To give the old man time to recover, he picked out six cigarette-holders and laid a note on the counter in payment. Mr Hamble violently blew his nose.

'That's all,' he said abruptly. 'I never so much as riddled through the ash. I hadn't the heart. In a day or two they came round, those students, full of regrets and explanations. I wouldn't listen to them. I sold the business, moved here, set up as a tobacconist; and I've never prospered since. I expect,' said Mr Hamble, 'I haven't had the heart.' He looked at Sherrard earnestly. 'Now, as a man of education,' he said, 'and a man of the world – what d'you make of it?'

Sherrard hesitated.

'It's certainly a remarkable story,' he said. 'It's one of the most remarkable stories I've ever heard.'

Mr Hamble moved his big shoulders impatiently.

'I know *that*,' he said. 'What I mean is – looking back over the whole matter – for I am always looking back over it – would you say I had been fooled?'

'Fooled?' repeated Sherrard.

'I gave him,' said Mr Hamble, almost shyly, 'a lot of affection. One doesn't like to be fooled in one's affections.'

Sherrard took a moment or two to think this over.

'If it's any consolation,' he said at last, 'I don't believe your case is unique. A good many men have a bear of sorts.'

'I never heard tell of another,' said Mr Hamble jealously.

'Not an actual bear, as yours was. It may be a golf-handicap, or land, or stamps, or Basic English. With women it's very likely to be a house.'

Mr Hamble pondered.

'I take your point,' he said. 'I once knew a man ruined a very nice little business collecting pewter snuff-boxes. Ugly clumsy things they were. No one wanted them, and he wouldn't have sold if they had.' Mr Hamble shook his head. 'But affection,' he said, 'is different.'

'Put it another way,' said Sherrard. 'The French say that in every love affair there is one who kisses and one who is kissed. Many people believe that the one who kisses has the best of it.'

Mr Hamble looked at him shrewdly.

'And what,' he asked, 'may be *your* bear?'

Sherrard counted his cigarette-holders; six of them, at half-a-crown each.

'My bear,' he said, 'has golden hair and brown eyes, and is unshakeably faithful to the memory of her late husband. Shall I catch my train to go up to Scotland to have lunch with her, or shall we both go out and get a drink?'

It took Mr Hamble an appreciable time to answer, and even then he did not do so in words; but he reached up to a peg behind him, and from it took down a small Homberg hat.

George Lambert and Miss P.

GEORGE LAMBERT was a man who liked to take holidays, and circumstances combined to gratify his taste. Though a spasmodic worker, needing long periods of relaxation, he possessed in the field of electrical engineering such brilliant and profitable talents that his firm, besides paying him an ample salary, readily allowed him frequent leave. He had no wife to double expenses, and he had a secretary to save him all trouble. Miss Parker, (always referred to by George as My Miss P.), bought tickets, made reservations, told him which 'plane he was catching and whether he should pack a dinner-jacket; and had moreover, in the course of their association, developed such a remarkable nose for hotels that George was never let down at his destination. Give Miss P. half-a-dozen identically lyrical brochures, and she would unerringly pick out that which most closely approximated the reality. If Miss P. promised George there would be dancing, there was dancing – and to a first-class orchestra; if she assured him the cuisine would be genuine Provençal, George battened on *tarte aux oignons*. Her powers of divination extended even over the weather: if she told George there would be snow, there was. Miss P. herself never ventured further than Dorset, to a summer camp; had George ever thought about it he would have assumed that she enjoyed packing him off to Sweden or Majorca or the Canaries – always by the best route and to the best hotel – simply as an exercise in virtuosity.

As a matter of fact, Miss P. was so completely invaluable to George that he never thought about her at all. He paid her, or rather his firm paid her, an evidently adequate salary, and in return Miss P. (besides organizing his holidays) did all George's routine work, deciphered his scrawls, saw his drawings through the print-room, provided doughnuts for his tea, and dropped an iron curtain over his meditations. George simply found conditions tolerable. He had never had to do without Miss P., because she always took her holiday while he was taking one of his.

None the less, as he sat dining on the terrace of the Rosario, George Lambert spared Miss P. a grateful thought. Hotel and grounds occupied almost the total area of a small Mediterranean island, and the situation was superb. Wherever the eye turned blue sky met blue sea, broken only by the green and rose, or green and gold, of oleanders and orange-trees. The building itself was washed a dim, tactful pink. There was a bath to every room, and the food was as perfectly simple as money could buy. Moreover – George was something of a holiday philanderer – George had already marked, at a table not far from his own, a charming little creature as solitary as himself.

Miss P. had assured him there would be dancing: there was. The twanging mandolins were first-class of their kind, and in the situation not to be improved on. In plain English – George always found this the best approach – he invited the charming little creature to dance. She accepted. She was Italian, she was a Contessa, she had a disagreeable old husband in Rome; so far George's plain English (hers was prettily broken), took him that first night; he went to bed extremely pleased with himself, with the Rosario, and with Miss P.

He did not feel nearly so pleased when the following afternoon, coming up from the diving-rocks, he met Miss P. coming down.

He almost failed to recognize her; it would have been excusable. In the office Miss P. always wore black or navy-blue, high-collared with white. She now wore a bright yellow bikini. In the office Miss P. always wore glasses; she did still, but they were the universal sun-glasses of the coast. No wonder George stared. No wonder that for some seconds he doubted his eyes. When he looked at Miss P.'s navel, he disbelieved them altogether. In fact, as he went on up the path, he decided he'd been mistaken.

By evening, however, he could deceive himself no longer. Dressed for dinner, in neat and appropriate organdy, white with navy trimmings, Miss P. was unarguably Miss P. She sat at a table for one, apparently enjoying both her dinner and the view; she looked very comfortable. George, on the other hand, was beginning to realize why his sub-conscious had fought so hard not to recognize her. There are times when a man wants his secretary around, and times when he doesn't. Consuming melon, George felt merely surprised; he also – a kindly chap at heart – feared Miss P. might be going to find herself a trifle lonely and out of things. But when the mandolins struck up after dinner, when he led his Contessa on to the dance floor, the full realization burst on him that Miss P. was going to be a damned nuisance.

There are times when a man wants his secretary around, and times when he doesn't. The moment when a Contessa's cheek lightly brushes his own is a time when he doesn't. The charming little creature, her gesture made, naturally awaited an answering pressure from George's arm. They were just passing Miss P.'s table. Of course George didn't give a darn what Miss P. thought of him, it was no business of hers, but her mere presence – trailing, so to speak, clouds of office memoranda – put him off his stroke. The Contessa pouted. 'Let's go into the garden,' said George. The Contessa shook her head. He shouldn't have said it till later. They finished the dance in silence, and the Contessa devoted the rest of her evening to a racing motorist. George had to hang about until after midnight, when Miss P. went to bed, before he could even begin to make up lost ground.

George didn't sleep very well that night, because he was thinking about Miss P.

By morning he was ready to take action. How often a problem needs only to be stated, to be solved! George knew, vaguely, that Miss P.'s holiday commonly lasted a fortnight. If she was going to spend the entire two weeks at the Rosario, George's own holiday would be ruined. But so – how could the solution have evaded him so long? – so would Miss P. The Rosario was quite fantastically expensive. However adequately salaried, Miss P. couldn't possibly afford it, her instinct for the best was obviously leading her into terrible difficulties. She wouldn't be able to pay. The hotel would fetch the police. Miss P. would be incarcerated, possibly for months, in some unhygienic island jail. It was George's plain duty to save her from this fate.

He was glad to find her with a beach-robe over her bikini. The decorous white towelling made her look more like his Miss P. With the kindest, if not the most disinterested intentions, George approached.

'Well, this is a surprise!' said George heartily.

'*Is*n't it?' agreed Miss P.

'I thought you always went to Dorset,' said George.

'I always *have*,' agreed Miss P. 'But just for once I thought I'd like to see one of the places *you* go to.'

George was touched. He might have gone on being touched had not Miss P. seen fit at that moment to cast aside her robe. She had quite a good figure, and she couldn't have been more than twenty-five. The Contessa, just then passing, cut George dead.

'I'm only a bit worried,' said George, 'about what it may be letting you in for. Financially, I mean. I mean, I don't know exactly what the firm pays you, but I do know what the Rosario costs –'

'The earth,' said Miss P.

'Exactly,' said George. 'I mean, I'm sure you can't afford it. I'm sure there are dozens of nice little *pensions* round Amalfi where you'd be much happier. You've probably booked your room here, but if you'd like me to talk to the manager –'

'I shall be able to pay,' said Miss P.

'Honestly,' said George, 'I don't see how you can.'

Miss P. gave him a very strange look.

'Wait till the auditors check the petty cash,' said Miss P.

George was so taken aback, George was so horrified and alarmed, that he simply sat where he was, mouth and eyes agape, while Miss P. rather gracefully rose and strolled down to the swimming-beach. He continued to sit and gape for several minutes after she disappeared. He had never been so upset in all his life.

If he hadn't heard the words from Miss P.'s own lips, George would never have believed them. If the whole office, if the whole Metropolitan Police Force, had accused Miss P. of pocketing the petty cash, George wouldn't have believed *them*. A bishop pocketing the collection was less unlikely to him. Only by Miss P.'s own statement – and the very peculiar look accompanying it – could his trust in her have been shaken.

To make matters worse, he didn't know what the devil to do.

Should he wire the office, and tell them to check the petty cash at once? How much was there ever *in* the petty cash? His notions of office procedure were so vague that he couldn't even guess the answer. Had Miss P. made off with fifty pounds, or a hundred? If fifty, George thought, he'd pay up out of his own pocket, just to save trouble all round. But suppose it was a hundred? Suppose it was more? Suppose the firm prosecuted? Suppose Miss P.'s jail wasn't after all the island variety, but Holloway? 'The girl's *mad* . . .' thought George.

He decided, however, not to wire. (He was always lazy: and he could hardly get Miss P. to wire for him.) He decided to make one more attempt to bring her to her senses.

'Look here,' said George that night, in the course of a rhumba, 'why don't you clear out to Amalfi as I've suggested, save whatever you've snaffled, and put it back before anyone finds out?'

'I want to see life,' said Miss P.

George released her for two stamping steps. He'd had to ask her to dance because she'd picked up with some Poles, and it was the only way of getting her alone.

'You'll get the sack, you know,' said George.

'At least I'll have seen life first,' said Miss P.

She was impossible. She was completely unreasonable. She also stayed on at the Rosario. For George in the end followed the line of least resistance, and did nothing. He decided to let Miss P. take whatever was coming to her, but in due course. If the only way of eliminating Miss P. from the Rosario was to have her flown back to England in custody, he decided to put up with Miss P.

Of course his own holiday was shot to pieces. It wasn't that Miss P. in any way kept tabs on George, on the contrary – and how naturally – she tended to avoid him. Nor was her general behaviour in any sense a reproach to his own – on the contrary again: as the days went by Miss P. picked up with more and more dubious characters, and freely entered into their fun and games. She certainly wasn't lonely, she certainly wasn't out of things; at the cocktail-hour one couldn't see Miss P. for Greeks. ('Because she's a free spender,' thought George censoriously. 'They probably think she's a millionairess ...') But the odd result was that as the conduct of Miss P. became more abandoned, so the conduct of George became more restrained. He felt, obscurely, that he ought to set her an example: he meant *his* behaviour to reproach *hers*: naturally his holiday was ruined.

Instead of pursuing the Contessa, he got into a steady, all-male bridge four. Instead of going to bed at dawn, he retired in good order at midnight. He played a lot of tennis with the pro., and helped coach a couple of small boys. He taught a female infant to swim. In no time at all every child in the hotel was addressing him as Uncle George. None of it had the least effect on Miss P.

Obviously George couldn't tell how she would have behaved *without* his example, he only felt she could hardly have behaved worse. (He thought about her almost continuously.) Her particular ally was an Italian, lithe and smiling, superb on the diving-board, and given to full-throated song in the small hours of the morning. He used to serenade Miss P. regularly. There was also a Greek who taught her poker, and a Pole who taught her Polish. Miss P.'s days were filled to overflowing, and as for her nights ... well, everyone hoped she got enough sleep. But she was certainly seeing life: her skin browned and her hair bleached, her figure got better and better, her spirits rose higher and higher, and she was known as the Blonde Bombshell.

At the end of ten days George cut his holiday short and went home. He had lost a good deal of money at bridge, he had tennis-elbow, and he was sick of being called Uncle George. He said good-bye to Miss P. only by accident; they happened to meet on the landing-stage.

'You're not *going*!' exclaimed Miss P., in surprise.

'Yes, I am,' said George.

'But you've still four days,' said Miss P. automatically.

'And I'm still going,' said George.

'Oh, well,' said Miss P. lightly, 'I expect one of the typists will look after you. Ask for Mabel.'

It was a slight return to grace – but how slight! Never before had she abandoned him, even for twenty-four hours, to the mercy of the typists. Never before had George returned from a holiday uncertain of finding Miss P. there before him. How could she now abandon him to Mabel? And in a wider sense, how *could* she? How could she speak so insouciantly, stand so insouciantly, browned and bleached and Bikini'd, knowing what lay in store? 'I could understand her not worrying about me if she was worrying about herself,' thought George, 'but, dammit, she doesn't seem to be worrying at all! *I'm* the one who's worrying . . .'

Once again George stared at her in amazement; and once again Miss P. gave him that strange, disturbing look. They stood thus for perhaps half a minute, neither speaking again; then someone shouted from the gangway, and George turned and walked up it.

He was to fly from Nice; Miss P. had assured him – only a fortnight ago – but how much can happen in a fortnight! – that this was far the best route.

As soon as George got back to the office he demanded an audit of the petty cash. It wasn't the right time and he could give no sensible reason, he simply said he was a bit worried about something; but he persisted, and he was invaluable, so they humoured him.

There wasn't a penny missing.

A couple of months later George Lambert told the whole story to a woman he was rather fond of. Mrs Cornish listened with great interest, and at the end laughed.

'My dear George,' said Mrs Cornish, 'it's as plain as the nose on your face. Miss P.'s in love with you.'

George was astounded.

'She wanted you to *notice* her,' explained Mrs Cornish. 'I don't suppose you ever noticed her in the office, you just took her for granted. So she followed you to the Rosario –'

'But it doesn't make sense,' interrupted George. 'Even if you were right, as I jolly well know you're not – why did she tell that thumping lie? It worried me no end.'

'She *wanted* you to worry,' elaborated Mrs Cornish patiently. 'Of course it makes sense. On your own showing, you spent your entire time noticing, and thinking about, and worrying over Miss P. You noticed she's got a good figure –'

'Very,' said George.

' – which you'd never noticed before, and you noticed that other men were attracted to her –'

'Because she bought them drinks.'

'Fiddle,' said Mrs Cornish. 'I've no doubt there were other women in the hotel prepared to be just as generous. *They* weren't known as Blonde Bombshells.'

George thought back.

'She did,' he admitted, 'look pretty striking in that Bikini. And certainly I noticed her. But your theory still doesn't make sense.'

31

'Of course it does,' retorted Mrs Cornish. 'Why don't you marry her, George? She sounds as though she'd make you a first-rate wife.'

George rather glumly emptied his tea-cup.

'She's married someone else,' said George. 'I'm trying to tell you. She left a month ago to marry this Italian chap. They're going to run an hotel. If *that* doesn't make your theory nonsense, I don't know what does.'

'Dear me,' said Mrs Cornish.

'You tell me she's in love with me,' persisted George, 'and she goes and marries an Italian. The office gave 'em a tea-set. What have you to say to that?'

Mrs Cornish reflected a moment. She did indeed look surprised, but her expression was changing fast. She finally, George thought resentfully, looked rather pleased.

'At least Miss P.'s holiday wasn't wasted,' said Mrs Cornish. 'All's well that ends well, don't you think?'

'No, I don't,' said George. 'It hasn't ended well at all, I'm still absolutely baffled, and what's worse, I've got to find another secretary.'

Mrs Cornish laughed and laughed. She laughed so long that George grew impatient.

'It's not so easy as you think,' he complained, 'to find someone who remembers the doughnuts.'

Thief of Time

I DID not as a child give much thought to such major abstractions as life, death and eternity. I hadn't the leisure: I had four brothers and a baby sister, a half-share in a pony, two Sealyhams and a fluctuating number of Belgian hares. In my tenth year, however (memorable also as the year when my mother gave up trying to make my hair curl and allowed me to wear pig-tails), circumstances forced me for some weeks to grapple with the phenomenon of *time*. These circumstances were of my own making, and the result of a crime: I had stolen fifteen minutes belonging to our esteemed friend and neighbour, Mr Rickaby.

Even today, forty years later, I am still astounded by the far-reaching consequences of my attempts to give them back.

Mr Rickaby was an elderly mathematician who had come to spend his declining years in our Dorset village. As a rule our village attracted retired Colonels: Mr Rickaby was a retired professor. He conformed, however, so exactly to type – being fragile, untidy and absent-minded – that everyone knew where they were with him; and I cannot better explain how thoroughly he was accepted, than by recording that the Marlowes of Old Mill allowed their daughter Cecilia to act as his secretary. In 1911 a secretary was rather an unusual thing to be, especially for a girl of good family; the Marlowes' family was so good, and so old, that they seemed to be fading away from sheer age and goodness. Cecilia's parents always reminded us children of the long, thin, shadowy-transparent figures in the stained-glass windows of our village church. They were vegetarians. Cecilia, though also long and thin, had more vitality, and what I see today as an instinct of self-preservation. She couldn't type, of course, but she wrote a very clear hand, and by dint of sheer concentration soon learnt to disentangle Mr Rickaby's notes, and copy out his mathematical formulae, with perfect accuracy. Mr Rickaby paid her twenty pounds a year, and after that the Marlowe's weren't quite so vegetarian, but of course it was thoroughly understood that Cecilia helped Mr Rickaby only because of her deep, though hitherto unsuspected, interest in higher mathematics.

I should never have guessed that anyone *minded*, had not my father one day made a joke about turning me into a lady-secretary too. My mother emitted a little wail of dismay, and impulsively unbraided my nearest pig-tail to see if there were any sign of curl.

'Mary will marry!' cried my mother – but with more defiance than conviction.

'Cecilia was no plainer at the same age,' observed my father.

'The Marlowes never had a penny to buy her a decent dress!' cried my mother – and hastily checked herself, because one never discussed money, especially before children. '*I* consider Cecilia extremely distinguished,' said my mother. 'And I hope we shall all be even nicer to her than usual, and certainly not make silly jokes – because I really don't know how the Marlowes can bear it,' cried my mother uncontrollably, 'seeing Cecilia go out every morning to *work for her living*!'

Of course I saw then how awful it was. At the same time I decided that *I* would work on a farm. This prospect didn't distress me at all, and I began to eat even more than usual, to get very strong. When people observed, as about this time they frequently did, that I ate 'like a ploughboy', I felt a secret triumph; my poor mother was openly chagrined.

2

It is always hard to estimate the length of child-time, but I believe that the scene of my crime had been set for at least a year before I committed it. Mr Rickaby had been amongst us that while, and I cannot think he went without his exercise for long. He was a man of most regular habits, and firmly believed that his health required a four-mile walk each day; but though on the face of it nothing could have been simpler – our neighbourhood abounded in walks, we children could have shown him at least three, the Pig Walk, the Boghole Walk, the Dangerous Stile Walk, all the right length – the very attractions such names defined were to Mr Rickaby positive draw-backs. He did not wish to dodge sows, leap bogs, or negotiate stiles. While walking he liked to think. He disliked even opening gates (which he usually forgot to shut), or having to watch out for the sparse traffic of our main road. In Cambridge he used to walk round and round a quadrangle. His cottage garden was so small that it made him dizzy. So he finally asked my parents if he might use our three-acre pasture.

I think my parents were rather flattered. Mr Rickaby, they impressed on us – we had a tendency to refer to him as Old Mouser, from a fancied resemblance to a departed cat – Mr Rickaby was a very distinguished person, who published books and contributed to learned periodicals. They readily offered our pasture; and thus it happened that any morning between nine and ten we could see from the schoolroom window

35

Mr Rickaby marching round and round exactly like a clockwork toy. It was my father who suggested an hour when we children were necessarily indoors; in holiday-time he put the pasture out of bounds for the same period. This did not, of course, prevent us from keeping an eye on Mr Rickaby all the same.

He had one fascinating idiosyncracy. Our pasture was about a mile round; Mr Rickaby had therefore to circumperambulate it four times. By way of keeping count, each time he passed the gate he picked up a pebble from the path outside and placed it upon the flat rail; when there were three pebbles in a row, and he held the fourth poised in his hand, he dashed all to the ground and went home. It always used to astonish us to see him quite obviously pause to check them, one, two, three, whereas *we* could have taken in the number at a glance, *en passant*. But Mr Rickaby, we were told, was a *higher* mathematician, not the low sort like ourselves, an explanation we endeavoured to accept.

He never entered the house, except on the first Wednesday of each month, when our parents invited him to dinner. (He used to fall asleep immediately after the coffee, and my mother would awaken him at the right time by playing very loudly on the piano.) But though he thus remained essentially a stranger, we children were on the whole fond of Mr Rickaby, as we were fond of the old lawn-mower pony, and I had certainly no wish to do him harm.

Indeed I well remember, that second summer, feeling unusually sympathetic to him, because he was under a cloud, as I often was myself. The root of Mr Rickaby's disgrace, however, was not appetite or argumentativeness, but simply his fame. If he hadn't been so famous, he would never have drawn Mr Demetrios to our village.

What a summer that was! – Mr Demetrios was so appalling that memory pauses, fascinated, at the very name.

3

I cannot honestly say I remember anything personally very dreadful about him: I see him fifty-ish, small, brown-skinned, with very dark, rather melancholy eyes. He was perfectly clean, and spoke English with only a slight American accent. His manners, in intention at least, were good. He still appalled us.

In the first place Mr Demetrios was a Greek, which was bad enough; in the second he was vulgarly rich. (It got about that he had made his money in New York, in a place called Wall Street. My father always referred to him as The Financier.) And besides being a very rich Greek, Mr Demetrios acted like one.

He wore an overcoat with a fur collar, and a diamond ring.

At the Crown, our only inn, he occupied a bedroom *and* a sitting-room, where he took his meals.

He hired an automobile, with chauffeur, to drive about the country.

He drank wine not only at dinner, but also at lunch.

He gave a hundred guineas to the church restoration fund, when even Sir Percival (at the Manor) gave only ten.

Of course no one took any notice of him.

To the general credit, Mr Rickaby was never accused of having Mr Demetrios for a *friend*. The village was in general agreement that Mr Rickaby would never have brought Mr Demetrios amongst us, had he known what Mr Demetrios was

37

like. But he had none the less *attracted* Mr Demetrios, and having done so – hence the cloud – actually tolerated him.

Today I appreciate Mr Demetrios better. He was an enthusiast. He was a man in prey to a passion – for higher mathematics. Other millionaires (and he was one) accumulated pictures and statuary, to perpetuate, in museums, their names and wealth. Mr Demetrios accumulated a narrow sheaf – just sufficient, in the end, to fill a narrow book – of mathematical fact. He had come all the way from Greece (or from America, no one bothered to find out which), to sit at the feet of Mr Rickaby. Enormous investments were going hang, tremendous deals were being botched, while he sat day after day in Mr Rickaby's cottage, drinking in from the fountainhead a thin stream of commercially-unproductive lore.

The village saw nothing of this. The village, though it already took a certain pride in Mr Rickaby's fame, turned an icy shoulder to his disciple.

I regret to say that we children at once conformed to the prevailing weather. I remember myself once encountering Mr Demetrios on the green, as he walked from the Crown to Mr Rickaby's cottage. He tried to engage my goodwill by offering me a peach. I recognized the fruit immediately – out of Sir Percival's greenhouse, the most expensive single items at a recent church bazaar. We had allowed Mr Demetrios to buy the whole basket. We had *expected* him to buy the whole basket. Sir Percival had sent a whole basket for Mr Demetrios to buy. But of course I refused. I raised a nine-year-old eyebrow, said thank-you-so-much, and turned to my heel with a fair imitation of my mother's best putting-off air. Today I can admire Mr Demetrios; even at the time I felt sorry for Mr Rickaby. I still conformed.

For Mr Rickaby should naturally have sent this outlandish

disciple packing. He didn't, because he enjoyed talking higher mathematics to someone who could understand him. The village thought it extremely selfish. Had my crime become public property, I should have had the village on my side ...

4

Why I was loose that fine September morning I cannot now quite recall. We did lessons again in September, and nine to ten was always Latin with the curate. Had I been arguing with the curate? It seems only too possible: I was a very argumentative child. Perhaps he had sent me out of the room: he was very young and painfully unresourceful in the matter of punishments. However, there I was, pounding down the lane – pigtails flying, still in my house-shoes – towards the big hawthorn brake that was always our first base. I had no notion then of making for the pasture: the hawthorns simply happened to neighbour its gate.

Under their friendly, thorny arms I paused for breath and looked about. On the other side of the pasture I saw Mr Rickaby – in his long black coat, diminished by distance, moving with his jerky stride, precisely the clockwork figure in the bottom of my last Christmas stocking. At that moment, I felt even fonder than usual of him. The moment after, my eye fell on the three smooth pebbles lying on top of the rail. Without the slightest premeditation I slipped the largest into my pocket and nipped back behind the hawthorns.

Mr Rickaby approached, counted, added another pebble to the row, and clock-worked on. I waited until he had turned the first corner, and then strolled over to the stable to talk to my pony. I felt, if anything, rather pleased with myself.

5

But not for long. Not, alas, for long! How clearly I recapture the moment when remorse first struck! It smelt of warm flannel. I was standing at the nursery door, taking a look at my baby sister: and there, directly opposite, over the fire place, hung a gaily-illumined text, *'Lost – one golden hour, studded with sixty diamond minutes. No reward offered, for it is GONE FOR EVER!'*

I must have contemplated that text a thousand times. It came into the family with Old Ellen, who nursed my eldest brother. We children had all grown up with it. We had used its ominous words for counting-out games. We knew them, and forgot them, as one knows and forgets the words of a bedtime prayer. Now they struck me with the force of a thunderbolt. Fifteen minutes – fifteen precious diamond minutes – had I stolen from Mr Rickaby; my heart turned over with an unpleasant thump; I recognized the symptom at once. Remorse was settling in my stomach like a lump of cold suet pudding, and I knew from experience that until I got rid of it I should feel no healthy appetite. I did therefore what I always used to do in emergencies: I told the boys.

For once they were no help at all. They regarded the whole thing as a good joke: I'd marched Old Mouser all round the pasture again, and the silly juggins hadn't even noticed. I regret to say that for some minutes I encouraged them. For some minutes I preened in their rare admiration of me. But for no longer. Remorse revived.

'Suppose,' I said, 'Mr Rickaby 'd been expecting some frightfully important visitor, and hadn't been there to meet him and he'd gone away again?'

'We'd have heard,' said my brother George.

'Well, suppose the postman came with some frightfully important parcel?'

'He'd have left it next door,' said my brother Arthur.

'Then suppose,' I cried desperately, 'Mr Rickaby'd been *thinking* of something – and didn't get home in time to write it down?'

'If anyone wants to come ratting,' said my brother John, 'it's six o'clock in the barn . . .'

So *they* were no help to me. I was vaguely surprised, vaguely injured. From that moment I date my instinctive sympathy with any movement for equal pay for women. (I wrote some secretary a cheque only yesterday.) I felt my menfolk had let me down – not through any lack of affection, or courage: I knew that if a village boy so much as cheeked me they would tear him limb from limb – but through lack of imagination. I was left to expiate my crime alone . . .

The worst part about stealing *time* is that it is so hard to give back.

On the surface, Mr Rickaby hadn't suffered at all. No important visitor, no important parcel, nothing of importance at all, so far as the village knew, had gone astray. Mr Demetrios never arrived at the cottage until eleven, so even he hadn't been kept waiting. Nor had the cottage caught fire. It seemed as though no quarter-of-an-hour since the creation could have been stolen with less ill-effect. My conscience still plagued me. We under-estimate – at least we under-estimated *then*, for these days of psycho-analysis I cannot speak – the dreadful force of a child's sense of guilt. I had done wrong, I was a thief; my appetite deserted me, I woke at least once, howling, in the night; and though it is true that this was after I had just picked at some cold goose, it is also literally true that I knew no easy moment for the next three weeks.

For the next three weeks, as a criminal haunts the scene of his crime, I haunted the proximity of Mr Rickaby. I dogged him about the village green. I peered each morning through his cottage window, as he discoursed within to Mr Demetrios, Miss Marlowe between them taking notes. Not one of the trio ever noticed me; I slunk disconsolate off. On the first Wednesday of the next month I crept out of bed and stole night-gowned down to listen at the dining-room door.

The ladies I knew to be already in the drawing-room: I had already marked their gentle swishing up and down stairs. (Does any child today, I wonder, recognize that soft, murmurous passage?) Around the broad mahogany, drinking port, only my father and Mr Rickaby, Sir Percival and the Vicar, still lingered. The door was not quite shut; its lock, in two hundred years, had never been put right. I applied my ear to the crack and frankly eavesdropped. The result was highly rewarding.

Mr Rickaby, who of course hadn't yet gone to sleep, was talking to my father about Young Barbarians. Today I guess that he referred to myself and my brothers; at the time I took him literally, and conjured up a rather pleasing picture of pre-historic Boy Scouts. I was interested. But Mr Rickaby did not elaborate: suddenly breaking off – 'After all,' he added nos-talgically, 'they *are* the best days. I'd give a great deal, sir, for another hour as a lad . . .'

A chair was thrust back, they were coming out; I scrambled upstairs again. But with what a spring of hope! For now I at least knew of something Mr Rickaby wanted. I might not be able to give him a whole hour – indeed, I didn't owe him a whole hour – but for some fifteen minutes, as far as lay within my power, I determined he should enjoy every pleasure my brothers knew. I wasn't yet quite clear how to set about it, but at least I had an aim.

As things turned out, opportunity beckoned the very next day. Precisely at eleven – for the church clock was striking – I happened to emerge from our gate just as Mr Rickaby crossed the green on his way from the Post Office to his cottage. I should say that our rural and picturesque green was bordered on one side by the beech-hedge of the Manor House: by ducking through a gap we children knew of (and had indeed made), it was a matter of seconds only before one reached (by nipping across a corner of lawn), the Manor woods. They were my brothers' happiest hunting-grounds.

Mr Rickaby and myself stood within a stone's throw of them.

As an embarrassment of riches, it was my day to have the pony. I could saddle him in two minutes timed by John.

The first thing, however, was obviously to corral Mr Rickaby. I pounded across the grass and placed myself in his path. He stopped at once, dropping two packages of books and a small loaf.

'Mr Rickaby,' I panted, 'would you like a ride on my pony?'

With an obvious effort, Mr Rickaby withdrew his thoughts from their native intellectual uplands and looked at me in such surprise that I felt, perhaps mistakenly, a need to elaborate.

'I share him with George, but it's Thursday. I have him Tuesday, Thursday and Saturday.' (It went without saying that on Sundays we didn't ride.) 'He's a very *strong* pony,' I added encouragingly. 'I'm sure he's up to your weight.'

Politely, but still looking startled, Mr Rickaby thanked me and said No. He said he feared the unusual exercise might prove too much for his old bones. But he had obviously taken the

43

offer in the right spirit; we stood contemplating one another with mutual goodwill. I felt I simply mustn't let him get away.

'Perhaps,' I suggested, 'you'd like to come for a walk instead? I know some very good blackberry-places.'

'My dear child,' said Mr Rickaby, 'this is most kind of you.' (He said it as if he meant it.) 'Unfortunately, I am even now expected at home. Had I a quarter-of-an-hour to spare –'

It was then I took the plunge, told a falsehood, and thrust his stolen fifteen minutes back into his hands.

'If you're going by the church clock,' I said, 'it's a quarter-of-an-hour fast.' And I added, really rather brilliantly, 'there's a man coming tomorrow to climb into the steeple and put it right.'

Without the slightest hesitation, Mr Rickaby believed me. Perhaps he wanted to. With middle-age I have myself learnt, how flattering it is to have my company sought by the young. When I seized Mr Rickaby's hand he made no demur; in two shakes I had him through our gap, across the Manor turf, and into the woods.

I did my very best for him. I crammed into that fifteen minutes the blackberry-place, the mushroom-place, the hollow tree and the Tinkers' Dingle. I let him find – myself acting pointer – the largest berries and the single mushroom. I got him right inside the tree, so that he could look out through the hole. I showed him how to read the signs the tinkers left. During a brief game of hide-and-seek – rather childish by our standards, but then I didn't know quite how young Mr Rickaby wanted to be – I allowed him to find me almost immediately, and never found him at all. And Mr Rickaby enjoyed it all. For once good intentions bore their designed fruit. When we emerged fifteen minutes later – for I kept an ear cocked all the time for the church clock striking the quarter, and added the last five by guess – he told me he hadn't enjoyed himself so much since he was a boy.

I hadn't either. The last three weeks had aged me; I hadn't felt properly boy-like – tomboy-like, ploughboy-like – since the fatal day I took his pebble. As we parted again on the green (his books and loaf were still there), youth surged back into my legs and I leapfrogged our mounting-block from sheer exuberance. My conscience was at last clear, my appetite returned, I raced into the house and ate three buns before dinner.

But what had been happening, during that same quarter-of-an-hour, at Mr Rickaby's cottage? It is almost too dreadful to relate.

Miss Marlowe, and Mr Demetrios, both arrived a few minutes early, thus missing the spectacle of Mr Rickaby and myself in converse. The cottage door being as usual unlocked, both went in. Both, equally surprised, though not to the point of alarm, by the absence of Mr Rickaby, sat down to wait. For fifteen – nay, twenty – minutes they were alone together.

It is difficult today to appreciate the rarity of such a situation. Miss Marlowe was a young woman earning, more or less, her own living. It was accepted that she might spend a couple of hours a day alone with Mr Rickaby. But then every one knew who Mr Rickaby was, and it was one facet of the Marlowes' confidence in him that they knew, without asking, that he would never place his secretary in any unladylike situation. Certainly he wouldn't leave her tête-à-tête with a person like Mr Demetrios. If she took notes in the presence of both men at once, the impersonality of the proceeding acted as a social disinfectant. But now Miss Marlowe and Mr Demetrios were together alone, and for twenty minutes; and how did Mr Demetrios employ them? By underlining every danger to

45

which Miss Marlowe might, but had hitherto never, bee exposed.

He made her, in short, a declaration.

With incredible obtuseness and audacity, Mr Demetrios, who had nothing in the world but several millions, invited Cecilia Marlowe to become his wife.

That was shocking enough. What was more shocking still – Cecilia Marlowe accepted him.

I still thank heaven that in all the ensuing riot no one blamed *me*.

For there was a riot, so far as the Marlowes could raise one. Before the prospect of so appalling a misalliance they and their connections roused themselves like a swarm of sleepy bees. Cecilia was reasoned with, browbeaten, sent away, brought back, set upon by titled aunts. Mr Marlowe called on Mr Demetrios at the Crown, and ordered him to quit our village. Mr Demetrios – pathetically prepared with a full statement of his financial situation – emerged from the interview to book his rooms for another month. For the first time within memory a landlord of the Crown stood pat to a Marlowe of Old Mill – we all felt the social system crack – and Mr Demetrios' booking was accepted. Mr Demetrios then went up to London and returned with an enormous diamond engagement ring, which Cecilia (receiving it by a suborned baker's boy), defiantly wore for two days. Mr Marlowe then, (so village gossip ran), actually wrenched it from her finger and returned it to Mr Demetrios in a match-box. My mother said Mr Marlowe had merely used rational arguments. In any case, Mr Demetrios got it back to Cecilia a day later, by suborning the postman, and she wore it again until Mrs Marlowe had a heart attack. Then Cecilia put it back in its case; but she still did not return it to Mr Demetrios.

At least it must be acknowledged that the Marlowes weren't mercenary: Mr Demetrios' money meant nothing to them. But then neither did Cecilia's happiness. One must remember the date – fifty years ago; I remember myself the horror of my own parents. Even my mother, for years lamenting Cecilia's lack of suitors, could see no happy issue. 'If only he'd been a gentleman!' wailed my mother; but that of course was the one thing Mr Demetrios was not . . .

It made no difference to Cecilia. She had glimpsed a wider horizon. With incredible, with unsuspected tenacity, she stuck to her guns. She was (I know now) twenty-seven years old; and if she couldn't marry Mr Demetrios with her parents' consent, she announced, she would marry him without. Even in 1911, one couldn't actually lock a daughter up.

With as bad a grace as possible, the Marlowes gave way. Mr Demetrios bought a special licence, and one morning, very quietly, in the village church – no choir, no organ, no bridesmaids – Cecilia became Mrs Aristide Demetrios. Immediately after the ceremony the happy pair left for London, where they stayed at the Ritz, en route for Paris, where they stayed at the Crillon. Cecilia's horizon was widening with all possible speed.

No one, as I say, blamed me. Mr Rickaby was blamed right and left, it was he who had brought Mr Demetrios to our village in the first place, it was he who by his incredible carelessness had given Mr Demetrios his opportunity; the Marlowes turned half their anger on him – but he never gave me away. We had it out together in private, one morning on the green.

'The church clock,' said Mr Rickaby, 'on the morning of the recent . . . ah . . . sensation . . . I don't think it could have been fast after all?'

I had had enough of crime. I decided to tell the truth.

'No, Mr Rickaby,' I said, 'it wasn't. I just told you it was because I owed you a quarter-of-an-hour.'

Nearly everything I said to Mr Rickaby seemed to astonish him. Perhaps this time he had more excuse than usual. As I plunged on, describing how I took his pebble in the first place, his bewilderment simply deepened.

'But what was your motive?' asked Mr Rickaby.

I mumbled that I didn't know.

'Had the pebble perhaps some childish value for you?'

I shook my head. Mr Rickaby looked at me uneasily.

'But you must have had *some* object?' he urged.

I said I hadn't. It struck me that if we went on like this I should soon have wasted another fifteen minutes of Mr Rickaby's valuable time. I said flatly.

'I'm a very *bad* child, so I expect it was just that. But I was sorry afterwards, and I heard you tell my father you'd like to be a boy again, so I made the quarter-of-an-hour the sort my brothers like. I did have a motive *then*.'

'And a kind one,' said Mr Rickaby.

He smiled. With immense relief I saw that he wasn't (unlike the usual adult) going to keep on at me. No doubt a man of his intelligence realized that there were some things it was simply no use keeping on at, like recurring decimals. He said kindly,

'I enjoyed our excursion very much, my dear. Don't meddle with time again, it's a subject for experts; but in this instance, I believe, we may say that all has ended well.'

I thought it wonderful of Mr Rickaby to take so broad-minded and sensible a view. Today I imagine that during the course of our conversation he had simply forgotten Cecilia Marlowe altogether. The notion of a child playing about with time – manipulating it, so to speak – must have been at once interesting and surprising to him. He never offered to teach me higher mathematics, but we were always, after that interview, very good friends.

7

Our village never heard much more of Cecilia Demetrios. Rather staggering presents used to arrive each Christmas at Old Mill; but neither Mrs Marlowe (in sable cape), nor Mr Marlowe (offering his friends superb brandy), spoke freely of their daughter. My own opinion of how the marriage turned out is derived from Mr Demetrios' autobiography, published in 1930.

I can't imagine that many people bought it. It is a dry piece of writing, nothing but a bald compilation of facts set down in peculiarly stiff-jointed prose. Only once, at the end of the chapter headed 'England', does emotion show through.

'It was during this visit,' wrote Mr Demetrios, *'that I met with the lady whose beauties of person and character, and whose quick intellectual sympathies, have ever since adorned my life. On the morning of October the fifth, 1911, seizing a long-sought opportunity, I successfully requested Miss Cecilia Marlowe to become my wife. It is a date that should rightly be printed here in letters of gold . . .*

I still have Old Ellen's text. The words there *are* printed in gold, except for 'sixty diamond minutes' in frosted silver, now a little bald. It makes an excellent book-mark, and I keep it in Mr Demetrios' book.

The Girl in the Grass

In CITIES, in summer, in fine weather, the parks become picnic-grounds. Clerks and typists bring out sandwiches, mothers and children from the suburbs unpack milk-bottles and hard-boiled eggs. Errand-boys drip ice-cream. Tramps ferret through ambiguous parcels. Elderly ladies, in couples, share cake and a thermos of coffee. Only the rich, through force of habit, continue to lunch at restaurants; and even they often stroll, and sit, in the park afterwards.

Mr H. E. Carstairs, (Iron and Iron Ores Consolidated), after lunching at his St James's Street club, decided to spend half an hour in the Green Park. Unlike the typists and the clerks, he could return to his office as late as he pleased. He found a vacant deck-chair, sat down in it, and opened his *Financial News*.

In cities, in summer, in fine weather, all the girls come out in cotton frocks. For about three acres all round Mr Carstairs the long, uncut grass was vivid with blondes in blue and brunettes in pink, nested to eat and chatter, or lying flat on their backs with their noses to the sun. Mr Carstairs noticed them generally, and impersonally. He wouldn't have recognized his own typist, and indeed wouldn't have wanted to. He must have read at least two columns of his *Financial News* before he noticed, as an individual, this one girl in the grass.

He noticed her because she was looking at him.

The power of the human eye is in this respect notorious.

Children sometimes make a game of it, staring till their unconscious victims, preferably adult, look uneasily up, and back. This girl, however, was no child, though her thin black dress moulded breasts and flanks and thighs small as a skinny 'teenager's. (Black: the dark unexpected note individualized her still further.) She was lying flat in the grass a few paces to Mr Carstairs' right. Her eyes were light, and long. When she saw Mr Carstairs looking back at her she dropped them; and a lock of tawny hair dropped too, hiding her whole face, as she buried it in the grass.

H. E. Carstairs turned to the American Market. For a moment he had actually felt flattered – and how absurdly, before what was no doubt a mere focussing of sun-dazzled eyes! All the same, it aroused in him an odd and unexpected nostalgia. 'Thirty years ago, when I was young . . .' thought Mr Carstairs. He in fact greatly preferred being successful and middle-aged.

When he looked up again, the girl was looking too. She had pushed back the tawny lock, and propped her chin on her fists, and this time, there was no doubt about it, her look was – admiring. Mr Carstairs turned to Company Topics. He wasn't a vain man. He hadn't, at fifty, a paunch, but that was about the most he'd have said for himself. At any rate he was quite certain he didn't resemble any film-star – so the girl couldn't have been after an autograph. What the deuce then *was* she after? Was she simply lonely? Casting a now wary glance over the top of his paper, Mr Carstairs marked several unattached youths within easy range. Perhaps as soon as he was gone she would turn her admiring gaze on *them*.

Yes, but why should she wait?

Mr Carstairs gave a mental shrug, folded his paper, quitted his chair, and went back to work.

2

His charming wife, that evening, in their charming home, for once rather irritated him. Two charming neighbours came in for bridge, and Susan Carstairs played so much better a game than her husband that her eye, if not her tongue, was constantly rebuking him. Aloud she said nothing worse than, '*Well*, old man!' – but Mr Carstairs found that irritating too. Brushing his teeth before the bathroom mirror, he told himself he wasn't as old as all that. He also told himself not to be a fool.

If the next day too hadn't been so extraordinarily fine he might have read the paper at his Club. He might, or he mightn't. In any case, the day was brilliant: the sun shone, the sky blazed blue, and after lunch – just because he *wasn't* a fool – Mr Carstairs again walked into the Green Park.

He didn't sit in the same place. Actually, there wasn't a vacant chair there, and neither he nor his suit was built for sprawling on grass. He had to walk all the way to the little baroque fountain – the one wreathed with crumbling true-love knots – before finding so much as an iron *pliant*. (In cities, in summer, in fine weather, all park seats are taken early.) There he sat down, and opened his paper, to enjoy a moment of solitude and tranquility, out in the fresh air.

He had just digested Notes on Iron and Steel when he felt her looking at him. She was lying about ten paces away, her elbows in the grass, her chin propped on her fists, and her eyes fixed on his.

This time they recognized each other. But no more than that; the girl didn't smile, or speak; no more did Mr Carstairs.

And she at least seemed perfectly content simply to lie there in the grass, and from time to time look at him, as – as a cat might look at a king. The image suited her: she was like a thin black cat, graceful only because she had graceful bones. One could almost see them, she was so skinny; more remarkable still, almost *feel* them. When she smoothed her dress, passing her small narrow hands over her small, narrow body, Mr Carstairs had the curious illusion that he too felt, through his own finger-tips, the small, bony protuberances that were her ribs . . . He passed quite close to her, as he left the park, but at a moment when she had her face in the grass.

That was on Friday. He had first seen the girl on Thursday. The week-end he spent gardening, under wifely supervision; but on the Monday he quite deliberately went back to look for her again.

3

For now began a most curious period, a sort of emotional excursion, in Mr Carstairs' life. He went each day after lunch into the park, and there sat some fifteen or twenty minutes, and each day the girl, now nearer, now farther off, but still as it were beside him, lay and looked at him from the grass. Mr Carstairs had no idea at all what he was doing. He had no idea what would happen, or even what he wanted to happen. He simply felt the girl's neighbourhood a sort of necessity to him. If he took slightly more trouble than usual over his appearance – went to the barber, for example, a trifle prematurely – he did so quite without thought. And if, on the other hand, he neglected to cut the customary rose for his buttonhole, that was done without thought also. Only Mr Carstairs' subconscious, which he never examined, could have explained that he wanted to keep his garden out of the park.

On the Wednesday, she spoke to him.

She was lying, as usual, a few yards from his chair. A vague wind-borne chiming marked some minute between the hours: the girl stirred, folded her slim thighs; rose, and wavered across the grass.

'I believe she's going to speak to me,' thought Mr Carstairs (Iron and Iron Ores Consolidated).

She was. In a soft, sweet, uncultivated voice she offered the classic phrase:

'Please could you tell me the right time?'

Mr Carstairs drew out his thin gold watch (gift from his wife on their tenth anniversary), and said it was a quarter to two.

Like a Japanese flower in a glass of water – like a lily under the sun – she seemed at once to blossom, and to collapse.

'I'd thought it was later,' she murmured. 'Thank you very much.'

And immediately she was curled in the grass again, this time so close to Mr Carstairs' left foot, that at the least movement he must have grazed her smooth, immaculate, virginal cheek.

Or was it?

The girl was now so very near to him that the shadowing of mascara round her light, now closed eyes, was distinctly apparent. She certainly used make-up; and Mr Carstairs was no fool. But how frankly she offered herself to his inspection! Mascara, and lipstick, had done what they could for her, but her small pale face was that of any city urchin – far from beautiful, not pretty even; at the most, touching . . . Her body was better. As Mr Carstairs had marked before, its very thinness gave it elegance, so that when she curled, she curled like a cat . . .

He heard himself say brusquely,

'Don't you ever eat lunch?'

She opened her eyes, and without otherwise moving repeated that movement of small, narrow hands over small, narrow bones.

'Not often. My sister-in-law gives me breakfast . . . Am I as thin as all that?'

'Haven't you a job?' asked Mr Carstairs. 'Can't you get one?'

She moved her head from side to side in the grass.

'I don't want a job . . . thanks.'

Well, that was something, thought Mr Carstairs. He was tired of people wanting jobs, and expecting him to provide them. At the same time, illogically, he felt an impulse to concern himself for this child. (Already on her face in the grass again. How easily distracted! Pushing her nose between the stems, like a cat in catnip!) Because she was too thin altogether, thought Mr Carstairs, remembering those small, sharp-edged ribs: a sister-in-law's breakfast, and for the rest of the day – probably buns. About to supply the address of a typing-school, he heard himself curtly inviting her to lunch.

'Meet me tomorrow, at one, at the Piccadilly gate,' instructed Mr Carstairs. 'Afterwards, we'll see what can be done about you.'

4

What the deuce had possessed him?

Several times, during the course of that afternoon, Mr Carstairs so questioned himself. What the deuce had possessed him? He wasn't in the habit of picking up girls in parks. This particular girl, moreover, was barely presentable. He would have to take her somewhere very quiet, or else very big, where she wouldn't be noticed. He didn't anticipate any rational conversation, and it certainly wasn't his business to find her employ. What then was it, what quality was there in her, that had made him act – and act for the past week – so thoroughly out of character?

The answer came, unexpectedly enough, as he was in the middle of dictating a letter to his secretary. Mr Carstairs paused for a word; Miss Brigg, her efficient pencil poised, waited cool as a cucumber and about as expressionless: and by the very absence of the quality in *her*, Mr Carstairs identified it.

Flattery.

Quite baldly, the girl in the grass flattered him. She flattered him by looking at him – or by not looking at him. There was flattery in her eyes, and flattery in her dropped lids: and in her voice, and in her whole bearing, passive, docile, female to his male. And women – thought Mr Carstairs suddenly – women *ought* to flatter; whereas they seemed to have forgotten how, there wasn't enough flattery going . . . Secretaries, for example, used to flatter their employers: they used to be virginal and devoted and inferior. Miss Brigg had a university degree and was engaged to a Civil Servant. She frequently corrected Mr Carstairs' grammar. Wives also used to flatter: they also used to be devoted and inferior, though not of course virginal: Mr Carstairs' own Susan not only played better bridge than he did, she also drove a car better – very minor points, no doubt, but ones constantly cropping up in their normal domestic life. Moreover, she was as efficient in her house as he was in his office, and for her age a good deal more attractive. How could she then, honestly, flatter him? Mr Carstairs admitted the dilemma, and at the same time recognized that flattery was what he wanted.

He didn't *want* rational conversation; he wanted flattery. He needed it. Like many another man with an excellent and competent wife, he was flattery-starved.

He became aware that Miss Brigg had very quietly laid her pencil down. Her gaze was now speculative – but not solicitous, oh dear, no! She wasn't going to ask if he had a headache, she wasn't going to run for an aspirin, she was just going to sit there and wait, despising him for a wool-gatherer, till he came back to business.

'Where was I?' asked Mr Carstairs.

'"The representatives who we shall send to Canada –"' replied Miss Brigg at once. 'It ought, of course, to be "whom".'

Mr Carstairs regretted his extraordinary behaviour no longer. He wanted to get back, as soon as possible, to the girl in the grass.

5

She stood him up.

She wasn't there, at one, at the Piccadilly Gate.

She didn't want, it seemed, to be given lunch, and then have something done about her.

At a quarter past two, Mr Carstairs ran her to earth near the bandstand. Literally to earth: she was lying quite flat, face downwards, buried in the grass.

The curious thing was that so soon as he arrived within a couple of yards, she looked up. He hadn't spoken, or called to her. She just looked up.

'I hadn't the right clothes,' she said at once.

Mr Carstairs, lunchless, looked down at her ironically.

'Did you imagine I was taking you to the Ritz?'

'No; somewhere quiet. Or big, where I wouldn't be noticed.'

He flinched. This was of course exactly what he had intended, but he hadn't meant her to realize it. Yet she didn't seem in the least resentful, her long grey eyes rather placated him. (Flattered him!) She said softly,

'You're so distinguished, *you'd* be noticed anywhere. I didn't want to let you down.'

Mr Carstairs was touched. He wasn't quite touched enough to sit down on the grass beside her, and there was no vacant chair, so he had to stand; but even this accident, by making him feel uncommonly tall, encouraged forgiveness.

'Another time, don't be so silly,' he said. 'I'll take you wherever you like.'

She hardly hesitated a moment. She might have been expecting those very words.

'Then I'd like to go into the country.'

'Into the country?' repeated Mr Carstairs – a little taken aback.

'You know,' said the girl. 'Where the evening's nice and cool . . .'

Now it so happened, by a peculiar coincidence, that on the next day, Friday, Susan Carstairs was leaving for a week-end visit to her mother. It was customary on such occasions for Mr Carstairs to give their cook a holiday by taking most of his meals out. His absence next evening would therefore scarcely need to be mentioned, far less explained. Mr Carstairs recalled all these facts instantaneously, and let opportunity call the tune.

'We'll go tomorrow,' he told the girl. 'But if you're not at the gate at six, I shan't wait.'

6

On Friday Mr Carstairs bade his wife a temporary adieu with rather more affection than usual, mentioned that he would dine out, and put in a full day's work at the office. He still didn't know what he was doing. Immediately, and this he wryly enough admitted, he wanted to be flattered about his driving. He wanted someone to sit beside him in the car. As a rule *he* sat beside his wife, even when conveying guests it was she who drove, because she drove so much better. Mr Carstairs looked no farther than a pleasant run towards the coast, and of course a pleasant run back. It wasn't till they had left London behind – for this time the girl was there waiting, she slid into the seat beside him like a little black cat – it wasn't until some twenty minutes after this that Mr Carstairs began to think even about dining.

It was obvious that they would have to dine somewhere.

Out of the tail of his eye – he was driving brilliantly but with concentration – he briefly considered the girl's appearance. She was wearing her thin black dress, no hat. Glancing down, he registered no stockings, high-heeled black shoes. He also registered, and this momentarily distracted him, an extraordinarily large handbag. For it was so unusually large, such a mammoth of a bag, that it might easily have contained all the girl's earthly possessions. More particularly, it could easily contain a brush and comb. It could easily contain a nightdress. In short, it might easily have been not a handbag at all, but the sort sold as 'Week-end.'

Mr Carstairs deliberately ignored it, and began a mental review of all possible dining-places on their route. He knew of several; most of them also knew him. He and his wife were rather fond, in summer, of a run out of London as far as the Bush, or the Crown, or the Castle Inn. Mr Carstairs instinctively rejected them. They were too sophisticated, too elegant. Even at such humbler hostelries as the Dragon, or the Rose, (also on their route), he felt his companion's appearance might be embarrassing. She looked, away from the park, so conspicuously undistinguished . . . As they passed a large suburban store he toyed for a moment with the notion of sending her in to buy a cotton frock: but the implication of this alarmed him, and he accelerated rather rashly, forcing a cyclist into the curb . . .

'What's worrying you?' asked the girl gently.

How intuitive she was! How sympathetic! How quickly she sensed, and allowed for, a man's preoccupations! Susan Carstairs would quite simply have taken over the wheel. Miss Brigg would have preserved an icy silence. But this girl just – sympathized. Mr Carstairs looked at her kindly and merely shook his head, as though whatever worried *him* was naturally beyond her comprehension. She looked admiringly back.

'I expect you've a lot on your mind.'

'I have,' agreed H. E. Carstairs.

'I think men, the way they run things, are just wonderful.'

The grossest flattery is quite often justified. If a hero is heroic, why not tell him so? If a man runs an international organization more or less single-handed, why not tell him he's wonderful? Mr Carstairs' directors didn't; they just paid him a whacking great salary.

'My dear –' began Mr Carstairs; and paused, for it was the curious fact, and yet in one sense not so curious, that he didn't know the girl's name. He hadn't, to be honest, wished to tell her his own. But if they were to spend the evening together the situation was obviously impossible. 'By the way,' asked Mr Carstairs, 'what's your name?'

The result of this very simple question was striking. Most people, asked their names, can answer without thinking. But this girl twisted round, one elbow over the back of her seat, and regarded Mr Carstairs not only thoughtfully, but expectantly. As though she expected *him* to supply the answer, to say 'Mary,' for instance, or Betty or Kitty or Pat, leaving her only to assent. And that this was indeed her attitude was shown by her next words.

'What would you like me to be called?'

'Sylvia,' said Mr Carstairs.

And if *she* didn't know why, he did.

7

'Sylvia!' called Mrs Carstairs – old Mrs Carstairs, H. E. Carstairs' mother – 'Sylvia, come and make up the doubles!'

The scene was a tennis party: in a vicarage garden: where H.E., then Harry, Carstairs, a gangling seventeen-year-old, beat the gooseberry-bushes for lost balls in company with the Vicar's daughter. She was young and beautiful and goddesslike; she subsequently married a curate. H. E. Carstairs never forgot her. He never forgot her name, nor, vaguely, that it referred to woods and meadows; and so now drew it up from his memory to christen the girl in the grass. Emotionally, it was about the rashest thing he could have done.

'Sylvia's pretty,' said the girl, quite content.

She didn't say anything more, she just sat silent and contented beside him, admiring his driving, contentedly watching the first wooded hillsides rise up to meet the swift-moving car.

And Mr Carstairs remembered a chalky cross-roads ahead, a village and a village inn; turned off between hedges, and some ten minutes later halted.

8

The inn was so small that it offered only one bar: the Public. Behind, cyclists refreshed themselves at a hastily-cleared family table. Above, one spare bedroom (double), offered modest accommodation to bona fide travellers. On this occasion it was untenanted. This the inn-keeper's wife made quite clear. She wasn't, she explained, a fussy woman, and cars did break down. Or sometimes they ran out of petrol . . .

Mr Carstairs and the girl Sylvia ate their dinner in the ragged orchard. If the orchard was an orchard, the dinner was a dinner. Barren branches, but decorative with small leaves, canopied their table; the sausage-like meat was nameless, but the lettuce crisp. In any case, the feast Mr Carstairs sat down to was not of food, but of flattery.

Hitherto, it will be realized, he and the girl had enjoyed no sustained conversation at all. They hadn't conversed in the park, their luncheon date hadn't taken place, and the drive down has been reported almost in full. Now Mr Carstairs was hungry.

'Tell me,' he began, 'why you looked at me like that, the first time, in the park.'

The girl Sylvia's long grey eyes spoke for her before she answered. They glanced up, then dropped – almost as though what they saw dazzled them.

'I thought I'd like to know you. I thought . . .'

'Yes?' prompted Mr Carstairs.

'I thought you looked so distinguished . . .'

She had a way of letting her sentences trail off, of leaving them, so to speak, to echo. Or to hover, like the smoke from a cigarette, just colouring the air. The adjective 'distinguished' so hovered now, under the apple-trees. But she didn't go on; she took up and nibbled a little heart of lettuce; and Mr Carstairs had to prompt her again.

'But didn't I seem as old as the hills to you?'

Sylvia chewed, and swallowed.

'I like older men best . . .'

Mr Carstairs was jarred. It was the plural that jarred on him. But how perceptive she was! Immediately, she added, 'Not that I know any men, really. I just thought *you* . . .'

'Yes?' said Mr Carstairs.

'I just thought *you* looked so distinguished, and experienced, I just thought I'd like to know you.'

With a first faint stirring of unease he realized that her vocabulary was unusually limited. Their conversation was becoming circular, somehow or other they would have to progress, they would have to get on; he also realized that any break from this limited (though undeniably flattering) round could be only . . . well, in one direction or another. Upstairs or down, in fact: down meaning back to the car. Upstairs there was a room, there was a landlady who wasn't fussy; there was Sylvia's mammoth handbag, there was also, he now remembered, in the boot of the car, a bag of his own packed for golfing week-ends. But the sum of these factors didn't include his own desire. He desired flattery; and it was beginning to seem as though his palate for the stuff was finer than he'd realized . . .

The girl, watching him – she was certainly perceptive, she knew what to do – put out her small, thin hand and touched his own. Her fingers were more eloquent than her tongue: they

nestled into Mr Carstairs' palm, a mere weightless handful of
bones, as though he held a bird there; and like a bird they were
tremulous, between confidence and alarm. What did it matter,
thought Mr Carstairs, that she wasn't particularly articulate?
Wasn't there enough flattery in her eyes, in her fingers? Wasn't
it, perhaps, her very sincerity that tied her tongue? (The first
Sylvia too, the girl in the vicarage garden, had been shy and
silent; Mr Carstairs found it easy to transfer some of her other
attributes as well to this second Sylvia, in the orchard.) He
looked down at the hand still lying in his, and with their first
gesture of intimacy, squeezed it.

'Oh, Mr Carstairs!' said she.

9

He let her go, he reined back, so abruptly that the table rocked
He said brusquely, 'How do you know my name?'

She dropped her eyes. But it didn't seem to him, just then,
quite so touching a trick.

'I just knew . . .'

'You mean you've known all along?'

'I s'pose so . . .'

'Either you did or you didn't,' said Mr Carstairs curtly. It
was as though he already foresaw all the rest, he was already
wounded to the quick. 'We'll presume you did. How?'

The girl sighed. No doubt she was disappointed too.

'My boy-friend works in your office. He took me to the
Christmas party. 'Course, *you* didn't notice *me* . . .'

H. E. Carstairs threw a backward glance over a gaggle of
young women, mostly in pink taffeta, and acknowledged that
he hadn't.

'But *I* noticed *you*,' said the girl.

It seemed to Mr Carstairs merely reasonable. At the office party, naturally everyone noticed him. He continued the cross-examination.

'All right. So that's why you – pursued me – in the park?'

She nodded. The wave of tawny hair dropped and hid her eyes. Mr Carstairs no longer found this trick touching either.

'All right,' he repeated. 'Why?'

'I thought I could make a friend of you . . .'

'And then?' prompted Mr Carstairs remorselessly.

'Oh, *well*,' said the girl, 'I thought, *if* I made a friend of you, you might give Robbie a rise.'

So there it was, the complete and banal and humiliating picture. Mr Carstairs didn't doubt it for an instant: he'd been subject to lobbying before, though on a rather different level: and if his brain, for the last week, hadn't somehow ceased to function, might have scented just some such motive from the start. It was he, by gum, who'd been the touching character! The babe in the wood, the babe in the park! How far the girl would actually have gone he didn't know, and didn't want to; all he wanted, now, was in the first place to conceal his wound, and in the second, to get back to London.

'Robbie?' he repeated coolly. 'What's the rest of his name?'

'Robinson,' said the girl. 'In the office.'

Mr Carstairs' brain, when functioning, enjoyed the resources of a card-index. He now recalled, in every detail, young Robinson's appearance, qualifications and record. They were all slightly below average.

'My dear child,' said Mr Carstairs briskly, 'he hasn't a hope. Look farther, and you can hardly fare worse. Now finish that unpleasant food, and I'll drive you back to town.'

He carried it off: he carried it off pretty well. But how flat, how sordid an ending to his excursion! They drove back in silence, each as glum as the other; in a sense unaware of each other, being both given over to no doubt equally unsatisfactory reflection. But the girl had at least had her run into the country, at least she could console herself with that. All Mr Carstairs could think of, in the way of consolation, was a strong whisky, and then, with luck, dreamless sleep . . .

'Where can I put you down?' asked Mr Carstairs, as they re-crossed the river. 'Where can you get home from?'

'Any 'bus stop'll do now,' said the girl resignedly.

He didn't enquire further, but halted at the next, let her slide out, nodded her good-bye, and drove on towards his own empty house. He too felt empty: spiritless, and tired, and a good deal of a fool. He was thinking, in fact, very little of himself, was H. E. Carstairs, Iron and Iron Ores Consolidated, as he garaged his car, and slammed the garage doors, and walked up between the rose-bushes towards his empty, unwelcoming house.

His key – how inevitably, he should have expected it – jammed in the lock. But before he could free it, someone opened to him. It was Susan, his wife; she must have been standing ready.

10

H. E. Carstairs stared at her so blankly that she retreated, just a pace or two, brushing the big jar of roses on the hall table. And her voice, saying, 'Harry?' held an odd note of enquiry, as though his look made him half a stranger.

'I dined out,' said Mr Carstairs automatically. 'I thought you were going to your mother's.'

66

'I was. I changed my mind.'

Mr Carstairs stumped past her into the hall and shied his hat towards its peg. He didn't know whether to be pleased or not. He'd promised himself a good stiff whisky and a dreamless sleep. He decided he wasn't pleased. He said discouragingly,

'You mother'll be disappointed. Have you 'phoned her?'

'Of course.' Susan Carstairs stooped to pick up his hat, which had missed the peg, and stood holding it between her hands. Mr Carstairs stumped on into the dining-room and poured himself his promised whisky. Everything else had gone wrong, but at least his sleep might be dreamless ... Over his shoulder,

'Well? What stopped you?' he asked. 'Why didn't you go?'

'Because of you, of course,' said Mrs Carstairs, following him.

He turned and stared at her again.

'Because of *me*?'

'Of course. Because I didn't know what was upsetting you. I just knew you were upset, and I didn't want to leave you all alone.'

Mr Carstairs could hardly believe his ears. He had to empty his glass before he could reply. Then he said, incredulously,

'D'you mean you *noticed* anything?'

'Of course,' said Susan Carstairs again. 'It started – didn't it – the Thursday before last. When we had the Bakers in for bridge.'

Mr Carstairs, refilling his glass, narrowly avoided an overflow.

'D'you mean you *noticed*?' he repeated – with rising hope.

'Of course I noticed! If you can't tell me, Harry, don't. But don't think, either, that I didn't notice.'

'I didn't think you noticed me at all,' stated Mr Carstairs

flatly. 'I thought you'd stopped. I imagined myself just a necessary, though unnoticeable, factor in this highly desirable residence.'

Opening her hands in a gesture of entreaty, Susan Carstairs let his hat fall, with a soft thud, upon the delightful blue carpet of their delightful dining-room. Until that moment neither of them realized that she still held it. But now it dropped, rolled, vanished; and with the hat went her self-control.

'When you wouldn't even take your rose!' wailed Mrs Carstairs. 'When I picked it for you, because I thought you'd just forgotten, and you still left it behind! And when you had your hair cut three days early! When you said good-bye to me this morning, at breakfast, as though I should never see you again! Of course I *noticed*! I notice every darn thing you do, and every darn breath you breathe, and you're so much my whole darn life I'm scared to let you see it, in case I grow into a darned clinging pest! But if you've fallen for another darn woman, I'll darn well wring her neck!'

Mr Carstairs had never been so flattered in his life.

Half-incredulous, almost shocked – for upon the lips of his Susan the expletive 'darn' equated the best efforts of a Marines sergeant – almost shocked, then, half-incredulous, but above all flattered. Mr Carstairs none the less set down his glass quite steadily – as a superior male should – before advancing to reassure his wife in the traditional masculine style. Taking his Susan into his arms, he told her not to be a silly little fool. Assuring her of his utter fidelity, he none the less spared breath to explain how opportunity, not merely during the past week, not merely beckoned, but actually pestered a man of his qualities. He couldn't, since his wife knew her, actually present Miss Brigg as a Helen of Troy; but he did present the girl in the grass, the girl he'd taken out to dinner, as a film starlet.

No doubt the gods of matrimony forgave him.

'Yes, but where is she now?' demanded Mrs Carstairs jealously. 'At the Ritz, waiting for you to dress?'

'I sent her home to her mamma,' said Mr Carstairs – quite probably speaking the truth.

'If you hadn't –'

'Susan!' said Mr Carstairs firmly. 'Stop!'

She stopped. She was a small woman. She played much better bridge than he did, and drove a car much better, and ran her house as well as he ran his office, and for her age was much better-looking; none the less, standing so close beside him, her head practically on his chest, she was small. And Harry Carstairs expanded his shoulders, and offered her security and protection, and was her husband and her prop and her all.

He felt like the man in the fable, who went to see the moon rise, and who after long climbing looked back, from the opposite crest of the valley, upon his own house, already silver.

Interlude at Spanish Harbour

IT IS no use trying to commit suicide in the waters of Spanish Harbour; the islanders swim too well. Toss a sixpence from the jetty, and two or three lithe young ruffians will be tumbling after it before it touches bottom; while at any larger splash, as of a falling body, the whole quayside wakes to instant life. Once or twice in each season (if the luck is good) some careless or careworn stranger will miss his footing, and then the lucent water boils milk-like with expert rescuers. The first half-dozen or so clutch at his helpless limbs, the rest content themselves with outlying portions of his raiment, and though the stranger may be a strong and resolute swimmer, he has no opportunity of proving it. Within ten seconds he is seized, saved, and hauled back to shore, there to be dunned, in several different patois, for extortionate rewards. George Cotterill, who lived on the island, once worked out some very interesting statistics; the least anyone had ever got away with, he said, was about twenty-two and sixpence at the normal rate of exchange.

In spite of this drawback, however, Spanish Harbour is a pleasant place, and the strangers continue to come. There is no hotel, but all round the bay stand tall old houses of white adobe, houses that turn their backs to the street and their windows to the sea; and these houses the strangers rent. The water in the bay is a clear jade colour, very different from the deep true Mediterranean to be seen from the roof-tops; but though many of the English bathe there daily, they all employ in addition, a shallow tin pan. What the other inhabitants do is not so certain; quite possibly they just have a sponge-down.

But then the islander, as young Foley observed, is not like your Anglo-Saxon. It was a remark he made frequently, and there was nothing odd in that. But what was exceedingly odd was the fact that, unlike most of his compatriots, Maurice Foley spoke not in sorrow, but in admiration. He admired the islanders' indolence, their lack of public spirit; he approved beyond measure their extremely individual attitude towards the sanctity of human life, which indeed they seemed to create and to destroy with equal insouciance; he liked their indifference to the suffering of animals. All that, he said, was excellent. It gave him great pleasure, he said, as he looked out over the island in the evening cool, to reflect that not one single inhabitant thereof was thinking about municipal reform.

To reflections such as these, and to very many others, the English on Spanish Island lent first a polite, then a perfunctory ear. They had their own affairs to attend to, and most of the men were over thirty-five. At that age, however agreeable the reminder of one's own salad days, one does not wish to re-live them. So Cotterill offered no objections, but simply returned to his painting, and the other two artists did likewise. There were always artists at Spanish Harbour, just as there were always one or two couples politely supposed to be on honeymoon. For the colony, though without either a lending library or an English tea-room, had certain compensatory advantages. It was widely tolerant. You took one of the white houses and did as you pleased in it. No one asked questions.

In all the island only four persons played bridge. They were originally only three, and the fourth had to be specially imported. Cotterill sometimes played draughts with the waiter at the big café, and at the other café, the little one, a tall Scot called Macintyre who came for an annual month played chess with the proprietor. For exercise one swam, and at night, on the stone quay, the islanders sometimes danced to the music of a concertina.

One other point must be mentioned. Wherever, between an island and the mainland, a steamer plies daily, the inhabitants of the island will gather on the jetty to watch her come in; but at Spanish Harbour, where the boat calls only twice a week, this is not so. Not a step – such is the strength of their indolence – not a step do the islanders stir. And thus it happened that the first time Cotterill saw the Foleys was not till the morning after their arrival, when he and the waiter were sitting over their draughts at one of the café tables. The Foleys approached, wavered, and finally sat down, so that the game had to be suspended and Cotterill was annoyed. Most people at Spanish Harbour would have had the manners to wait.

They were brother and sister, the boy about twenty-two, the girl perhaps five years older. They had the same nose and forehead, the same short upper lip; but the difference in colouring was so startling that no one would have thought of calling them alike. Maurice Foley was almost an albino; his hair, of the palest ash-blond, showed perceptibly lighter than the skin of his temples. Nor was this in any way due to sunburn; on the contrary, his skin, exceptionally fair and smooth, looked as though it would flush easily but tan scarcely at all. His sister was dark. Dark hair, dark eyes, a clear brown complexion. With a little more colour, thought Cotterill, she might have been lovely. And as the thought passed through his mind, she reached up and pulled towards her a spray of climbing geranium, so that the dark scarlet petals lay close against her cheek; and Cotterill's thought was justified. Then her brother spoke, she let the branch spring back, and a moment later their drinks appeared.

It does not take long, on Spanish Island, for the original inhabitants to know all, or all they want to know, about any newcomer. In the course of the next few days it was rapidly established that Miss Foley's name was Diana, that she and her brother had no other relations, and that they were travelling about Europe (as they had travelled for the last three years) in search of a climate which should at once soothe Maurice's nerves and stimulate his genius. For Maurice Foley was a poet; he had published two books of verse and a lyric tragedy. No one on Spanish Island had ever heard of them, but he himself said they were good. (The Scotsman Macintyre, on the other hand, to whom Miss Foley lent the works, said that they were bad; but then Macintyre had been brought up on Burns, with a side-glance towards Shakespeare.) There was also, just to complete the picture, a rumour of an unhappy love-affair, but whether Diana's or Maurice's nobody seemed to know.

Like all other visitors, the Foleys took a tall white house with a terrace over the bay. In addition to the terrace, it had a garden of orange trees, for it was one of the oldest on the island; and here, with the help of a very old woman called Carmena, Diana Foley set up house. She dusted the big bare rooms, and filled them with flowers; she went daily to the market (the old woman attending) and bought figs and grapes and peculiar-looking fishes. It was charming to see her; she moved down the line of stalls with such grave attention, now pausing to consult with Carmena, now hurrying on after a distant patch of colour, and all the while trying to hide her pleasure, to look matronly and severe, so that the stall-holders should not cheat her. They did cheat her, of course, but with a charm almost equal to her own – dropping a spray of pink

73

geranium on the short-weight olives, or gratuitously plucking an aged but still sinewy hen. Miss Foley didn't care. She had eaten *table d'hôte* for three years on end, and her fingers itched for a frying-pan.

In these mild pleasures Maurice naturally took no part. His life was full already. In the morning he wrote poetry, in the afternoon took his siesta, and at night wandered out to mingle with the islanders. He had, it will be remembered, a very high regard for them; but the sentiment was not reciprocated. The islanders, so far as they admired anything, admired physical beauty, physical strength, and the ability to carry liquor. They liked Cotterill, for example, because he could drink all day and walk straight in the evening. They liked Macintyre for his diving, and Diana Foley for her elegance. But Maurice Foley had albino hair and boneless limbs; after two glasses of wine he began to chatter like a monkey; and worst of all, he feared the water. He bathed sometimes, but he could not swim. So the islanders watched him with veiled contemptuous glances, and when he tried to address them feigned either deafness or imbecility.

But Maurice's sensibility was purely subjective. He continued undismayed, and whenever there was dancing always went down to the bay. He fell in, of course, and was vigorously fished out; but though the profits were inordinate (his sister, in a panic, disbursing nearly five pounds ten), the islanders were scarcely pleased at all. They disapproved of people who fell in during the dancing; the time for rescues was the morning, when there was nothing to be interrupted; and they were also repelled by the limp and pallid appearance presented by the rescued. Another person who was not pleased was Cotterill. Miss Foley's largesse, in its unexampled prodigality, had completely upset his statistics.

'That's the worst of women,' he pointed out to Macintyre, 'they can never keep their heads. Fifteen-and-six would have been ample.'

'It would have been a great deal too much,' amended the Scot dourly.

'Next time you talk to her,' Cotterill added, 'you might just explain things. Tell her that people are always being rescued, and that it's not fair to put the price up. She'll understand: she doesn't look stupid.' And with this advice Cotterill went his way and had a game of draughts. There was no real reason why he should not have spoken to Miss Foley himself, but such was his ingrained habit of mind – such his lifelong resolution to keep clear of women – that the notion never occurred to him.

If he would not speak to the lady, however, he was soon forced to speak of her; for Ian Macintyre, the best conversationalist on the island, seemed suddenly to have formed the inexplicable habit of constantly dragging her in. Whatever the subject under discussion Miss Foley's name was sure to crop up; and what made it all the easier was the fact that she had travelled so much. If Cotterill mentioned Mozart, Macintyre referred to Salzburg, and the month the Foleys had spent there. If Cotterill shifted to vodka or psychology, Macintyre followed up with Warsaw or Vienna. It got monotonous. And to make matters worse, the Scotsman's temper, usually so reliable, had begun to get very ragged. When Cotterill, for instance, idly remarked that such journeying must be very agreeable, Macintyre nearly jumped down his throat.

'Agreeable!' he almost shouted. 'Agreeable, you call it! A young woman of that age doesn't want to spend her life trailing about foreign countries! She wants to settle down, in a home of her own.'

75

'Then why doesn't she?' asked Cotterill reasonably. 'They seem to have plenty of money.'

'Because that unhealthy young cub won't let her. Because he's afraid that if she gets other normal interests she'll cease to bow down and worship. I could wring the little brute's neck.'

Cotterill looked up in surprise, for his friend was not usually so vehement; and what he saw surprised him still further.

'You've got a touch of malaria,' he diagnosed kindly. 'I get it still myself. You ought to go to bed –'

The Scotsman picked up a tube of ultramarine – he had found Cotterill at his easel on the cliff above the bay – and shied it into the sea. There was a splash below as an islander jumped after, and Cotterill grinned.

'That'll cost you more than a new one,' he said amiably.

'I don't care,' said Macintyre.

And now Cotterill was seriously alarmed; there was evidently more wrong than he had thought. But before he could ask any questions – or even decide not to ask them – his unfortunate friend had thrown reticence to the winds.

'The fact of the matter is,' said Macintyre, loudly and desperately, 'that I've fallen in love.'

Cotterill stared, swore, and stared again.

'With – with Diana Foley?'

'Yes. And I haven't a dog's chance.'

For a moment Cotterill sat silent, running a painter's eye over the man at his side. Tall, thin, sunburned, broken nose and well-shaped head – a better specimen than most, Cotterill decided; and though women in general seemed to prefer dummies, they were also notoriously ready to make the best of a bad job. The conclusion was thus rather favourable than not, and though with some inward misgivings – for his sincerest advice would have been to take flight on the next boat – Cotterill repeated it aloud.

'You're too modest,' he said encouragingly. 'Women fall in love with almost anyone.'

'That's not the point. As a matter of fact, I know she's – quite fond of me, now. But there's also that damned young brother. He stopped her marrying once, for which I suppose I ought to be grateful; and as soon as he realizes what's happening, he'll try and stop her again.'

'Then if she knows her own mind,' said Cotterill, whom the subject was beginning to bore, 'she'll walk out and leave him.'

Macintyre moved impatiently.

'No woman can leave a man who needs her for a man she's just in love with. And Maurice needs her all right; he lives on her like a parasite. Who else would bother to keep him alive, even?'

'But damn it all,' said Cotterill, 'she's not his mother!'

'Have you heard their story?' asked Macintyre grimly. 'No? Well, you'd better listen. They were left orphans when he was five and Diana ten. He was always sickly, Diana always strong. When the mother was dying she sent for Diana and told her that whatever happened she must look after Maurice. Those things make an impression. Diana promised, of course, and the mother died that same hour. The two children went to some aunt or other, a woman who had run mad on Theosophy and never remembered to order the dinner. If Maurice was to get enough to eat, Diana had to see to it. She did see to it. In a year or two she was running the house. The aunt didn't mind – she probably never noticed. Maurice was too delicate for school, so there was also a governess; and to save expense Diana didn't

77

go to school either. When Maurice was fourteen, he nearly died of pleurisy. Diana nursed him through it and literally saved his life. That made an impression, too.'

Cotterill nodded. He was beginning to understand.

'Five years later,' continued Macintyre, 'the Theosophist aunt died, leaving them a good bit of money. Maurice had drifted into writing, and wanted to travel. They came abroad, and they've been travelling ever since. Whenever Diana wants to settle down for a little, he throws a fit and says the climate doesn't suit him. If she wants to settle for good, he'll probably go paralysed.'

Macintyre ceased; and in the silence that followed Cotterill became aware of one outstanding fact. It was this, that until the affair had been settled, in either one way or the other, there would be no peace on the island. The immediate object, therefore, of all sensible persons, must be to bring matters to a head; so without further loss of time, and employing all the eloquence at his command, he began inciting his friend to rashness. Anything (he urged) was better than uncertainty; until the worst was known, no action could be taken to combat it.

'You mean,' said Macintyre, 'that I should go straight down to her this afternoon?'

Cotterill nodded. It seemed an awful thing to counsel, but what could he do?

The day that Macintyre's proposal was made known to him, Maurice Foley had a severe fainting-fit. He had it on a secluded reach of shore, where his sister found great difficulty in getting help. Almost beside herself with distress, she had to leave him senseless and run half a mile to the nearest habitation. Two islanders came back with her, and when they saw who needed their services were understood to remark that one would have been enough. The younger of the pair then flung Maurice

78

negligently over his shoulder, while the other lay down on the spot and gratefully went to sleep again.

It was a touch of the sun. Or that, at any rate, was Maurice's version; and as there was no doctor on the island to contradict him, he had his own way. For the next three days he kept himself recumbent and in darkness, while his sister, by the shaded light of a lamp, read extract after extract from his own works. He clung to her pathetically; he was like a little boy again. Her absence gave him a temperature, so that she could rarely leave his side. When her lover called she sent notes by Carmena, not daring to come down in person. Once Macintyre proved stubborn, and set himself to wait in the cool white-washed hall. After about twenty minutes a door opened and there were footsteps on the landing; but a voice called suddenly, the footsteps returned, and the door was shut again.

Late on the third evening, however, Cotterill, descending a zigzag path to the shore, remarked a man and a woman standing close together. Such sights, on Spanish Island, were so little unexpected that Cotterill did not even hesitate, but continued his steps until he was almost abreast of them. He then saw two things that disconcerted him: first, that the woman was crying, and second, that she was Diana Foley. She had her head on Macintyre's shoulder, and as Cotterill turned to go back he heard her sobs suddenly rise to a little desperate wail. She was calling on Ian's name, as though he was a person already gone from her.

The next moment, almost before Cotterill was in motion again, a skirt brushed his ankles and Miss Foley ran past. For an instant he saw her plainly, her white dress glimmering, her face pale as her dress, and round her head a white ribbon. The ribbon caught his eye. It seemed, in the midst of her distress, such a freak of fancy, so womanish in its frivolity, and then –

as fast did his thought run, whilst all the time she was still transfixed, as it were, in that instant of brushing by – he reflected again, and saw her tying the ribbon not in simple vanity, but because the time was so short. It was what a woman might do on her honeymoon, to surprise her lover with an unexpected beauty; only Diana Foley could not wait. So she had given him at once what he might not have time to discover; and like a lady painted by Lawrence – for so the ribbon revealed her – ran weeping up the path.

Cotterill turned again, for fear of overtaking her, and began once more to descend. Emotion always upset him, and in his instinctive desire to get away from it he forgot about Macintyre and quickened his pace. But Macintyre was still there, standing motionless in the shadow, and as Cotterill hurried past the Scot reached out and held him. It was the gesture of the Ancient Mariner, primitive and compelling.

'You saw her?' said Macintyre, thickly. 'She's gone back to her brother. She's got to give him his bromide.'

Cotterill said nothing. From below came the beat of waves, from above the sound of running; then the running died away, and there was only the sea.

'I believe he's a devil,' said Macintyre suddenly. 'Do you know what he said to her? He didn't ask her not to marry me, he's too damned clever. He asked her to wait until he's dead. And he'll die, he says, as quickly as possible . . .'

And now Spanish Harbour was disturbed. It was unused to having tragedy in its midst, and found the experience unpleasant. The islanders knifed each other, of course, but they were never tragic about it; the dead had peace (as the saying went) and the bereaved had the vendetta. As for the English on the island, it was precisely to escape all unpleasantness that they ever came there; and though such information as they had –

the mere broadest outline, as reported by Carmena, of a brother's objection to his sister's marriage – was not nearly so unpleasant as the whole entangled truth, it was quite unpleasant enough.

To do them justice, neither Macintyre nor Diana made any call for public sympathy, or in any way obtruded their sorrows; the harm was done by their mere presence. One sight of Miss Foley's face, one glimpse of the Scot's tall figure as he strode restlessly along the shore, was a sufficient reminder that unhappiness existed; and on Spanish Island unhappiness was out of place. It cast a blight. It put people out. Trade, pleasure, even the climate, all lay under the shadow of the Unfortunate Affair. No one went to the cafés for fear of hearing people talk about it; the big one put out fewer tables, the little one, deprived of Macintyre's support, put out none at all. Even the islanders were affected, and whenever they saw either Maurice, or Macintyre, or Miss Foley, hastily crooked fingers against the Evil Eye. The earnest desire, in fact, of everyone on Spanish Island, was that the whole trio should at once be shipped back to the mainland, there to work out their destinies in a less confined arena.

This, however, could not be, for Maurice Foley was still too weak to travel, and Macintyre (to make matters worse) seemed equally immovable. He had never before stayed longer than a month, and was now entering on his fourth week; but instead of packing his bags he bought a further supply of soap. He was going to wire to the *Morning Gazette* (he told Cotterill) for extension of leave; and such was the prevailing demoralization that for the first time in years Cotterill asked a direct personal question.

'I'm their news editor,' replied Macintyre. 'In another year I'll probably be editor-in-chief. It's as good as a seat in the

Cabinet.' But he spoke gloomily, almost absently, as though of ashes in the mouth; nor could all Cotterill's arguments shake his decision. 'If I go away now,' Macintyre kept repeating, 'I'll never see her again. That's a dead certainty. And as far as I'm concerned, she's the only woman there is.'

'But as far as the *Morning Gazette* is concerned,' asked Cotterill tartly, 'are you the only news editor?'

The Scotsman considered.

'Speaking from a thorough knowledge o' London, Scotland, and the Provinces,' he said at last, 'I should say I am. I have an exceptionally wide experience, and also what they call flair. Furthermore, I do not lose my head. Your solicitude is kind, Cotterill, but it will not be needed.'

So the message went its way, and for the next seven days the situation remained unaltered. Macintyre tramped the shore, young Maurice suffered, and Miss Foley shopped no more in the early-morning market. She kept to her terrace, which was indeed one of the pleasantest spots on the island, rising sheer from the water in front, and at the end from the stone quay, so that on nights of dancing one could sit as in a box over the shifting crowd below. Presently Maurice appeared there too, apparently a little recovered, but paler than ever after his confinement in the dark. He had been too ill to shave, and his lip and chin were covered with a thin albino down. The islanders, if he stood above the quay, turned their backs to the wall so as not to have to see him.

Maurice, however, did not notice. He was an injured, therefore a preoccupied man. For though his sister had voluntarily and finally surrendered all ideas of marriage, the victory was not yet complete. Macintyre still remained on the island: to drive him away was necessarily the work of Diana, and Diana, on this last vital point, was proving unexpectedly and cruelly stubborn. She would not order her lover's departure, she would not even request it, and on the plea that it would be too painful to both, was even refusing to see him. So Maurice walked the terrace in displeasure, looking now over the water, now over the quay, till little by little, as he looked and pondered, a plan began to shape. He was pleased with it from the first, but as things turned out the final, the finishing touch was not of his own devising. It was pure accident, and it was added, about three days later, when Diana slipped on the stair and twisted her left ankle.

They took their coffee that night to the sound of a concertina. The islanders were dancing, and when the islanders danced on the quay anyone on the Foley's terrace might quite well have danced too. But to neither Maurice nor his sister was the music inviting, Diana, indeed, could not even stand, and was lying with her feet up in a long wicker chair. Carmena had carried it out for her, and was now down in the kitchen making a tea-leaf poultice. She believed in tea-leaves for everything, did old Carmena.

'You needn't worry, though,' said Diana, moving her swathed foot, 'it isn't your China. I told her I thought Indian would be more propitious to me.'

But Maurice did not smile. He had not smiled for days. Diana dropped her head back on the cushion and for a moment closed her eyes. She was trying, as so often in those days, to shut out thought.

With a slow, reflective glance Maurice got up from his chair to lean against the parapet. He chose the angle between the two walls, so that looking down to the left he could see the quay, covered with dancers, and looking down to the right, the waters of the bay. The moment had come, and it tasted sweetly.

'Diana,' he said.

She looked up. Her foot was hurting her, making it difficult to smile.

'Diana, for the last time, will you send that fellow away?'

For a moment, in her surprise and pain, she showed such distress that he was almost afraid. If she gave the wrong answer if she yielded too soon, the plan would fall to pieces. That was not what he wanted. He wanted to carry it through to the end, to establish once for all unquestioned dominion. So with some show of passion, he began to abuse Macintyre.

'That damned fortune-hunting Scotchman,' he ranted, 'that damned penny-a-line hack . . .'

For the first time in their lives Diana looked at him with anger. Then she remembered that he was ill, and controlled herself to speak quietly.

'*No*,' she said.

There was a long, a heart-stopping silence. Then without another word Maurice thrust his foot into a crack and pulled himself on to the wall. In other circumstances, and with better health, he might have made a good actor; for by every line of his body, from the flung-back head to the nervous foot, one knew that here was a man who was going to kill himself. Diana knew it, too, and flung herself from her chair in an effort to run towards him. But just as Maurice had worked it out, so the scene unfolded. Her foot crumpled under her, and she fell impotent and tortured in a double agony. Then she began calling, imploring him, promising anything he wished; and at last, when he still stood unheeding, her cries turned to screams as she tried to summon help. Carmena was old and in the kitchen, there was music on the quay, but her terror gave her such strength that Maurice took alarm. If she went on at that rate, he reflected someone might quite well hear; so with a final glance towards the quay (where there were still plenty of people) he shook back his hair, squared his narrow shoulders, and dropped confidently into the bay.

But as Maurice himself had said, the islander is not like your Anglo-Saxon. He has no foolish illusions as to the sanctity of human life. When the dancers saw who had fallen, they were all extremely glad. They had rescued him once before, but this time they let him drown.

The Snuff-box

IN a window overlooking Piccadilly in the year 1923 two old men sat with a chess-board between them. Their game, the first of the day, was just drawing to a close, by which other members of the club knew it must be nearly time for lunch. In the afternoon, from four to six, they would play one more: and when the board was brought out in the evening a member could confidently set his watch at eight-forty-five.

'Mate,' said Colonel Paxton grimly.

They were both exceptionally bad players, but the colonel usually won. Like the British Army in general, he had great doggedness, whereas old Denis Groome could never fight to the end. It was one reason among many why they rather despised each other.

'You should have castled earlier,' said the colonel instructively.

Receiving no answer – and old Groome never did answer a remark of that sort – he began setting the board in readiness for their next game. It was always the colonel who did this, and his order never varied – first both kings, then both queens, and so to the last pawn. Old Groome watched sardonically. The sardonic was his attitude, which he had begun to cultivate as far back as the 'eighties, and partly from force of habit, partly from a natural bent that way, there was now no other emotion which he was able to express.

'See you later, then,' said Colonel Paxton, setting down the last pawn.

Old Groome nodded: the thought of lunching together would have filled both with horror. Leaving the board where it was – they had left it so for nearly ten years, and no one had disturbed it yet – they pushed back their chairs and went each his way, old Groome to the club dining-room, old Paxton to a certain chop-house. He had nothing against the club, only they couldn't do a floury potato.

The potato consumed, Colonel Paxton opened his paper. But he had read all the news at breakfast, and the advertisement columns, whither he now went gleaning, were not sufficient to hold his mind. It went harking back to old Denis Groome.

'I don't know why I put up with him,' thought the colonel fretfully . . .

Deep in his heart, however, he knew very well. Old Groome was his cousin: they had been boys together in the 'sixties, young men together in the 'seventies: he was now the only person alive who had ever called the colonel Nicky. Their years of maturity, indeed, had been passed poles asunder, by the colonel with the Indian Army, by old Groome between the stage and club door; but for the last ten years the retirement of one, the fading appetites of the other, and the bachelor-hood of both, had brought them together again.

'Force of habit,' grumbled the colonel, aloud. 'Force of habit and –' But the remark was never completed: his eye, wandering idly over Sales and Auctions, was suddenly caught and held by a long-forgotten, long-familiar name. Leonora Dupré! *The entire contents, including Valuable Oriental Collection, of 15, Elm Road, Maida Vale, formerly the property of Miss Leonora Dupré.*

'I wonder when she died?' thought Colonel Paxton. 'They didn't make much fuss about it . . .'

The minutes ticked by while he sat remembering.

Ever since they were small the two Paxton boys, Nicky and Bernard, had been told to give way to their cousin Denis. He had, it was explained, no kind father. That he had a recklessly kind mother, indulgent to every whim, was apparently neither here nor there. He had no male parent: and therefore the frequently-chastised Paxtons (whose own kind father was a martinet of the old school) were to let him break their lead-soldiers and borrow their air-guns. Nicky and Bernard obeyed, but their feelings towards Denis remained fixed and inimical. Ever since they were small, they simply loathed him.

Denis grew up rapidly. He never went to school, but studied at home under a succession of tutors. Mrs Groome, without being rich, had at any rate enough for her son and herself to live on, and there was never any question of his following a career. At the age of eighteen he simply stopped having tutors and became a man about town.

He looked the part perfectly. He had a long, thin figure, long, thin hands, and eleven pairs of trousers. His hair lay flat against his head. At evening parties where he was unlikely to meet relations, he frequently employed a monocle. As for the Paxton boys, Bernard the younger hated him still, but Nicky at nineteen, in the year he was cramming for Sandhurst, fell temporarily under his spell.

For Denis knew actresses. He was a stage-door johnny. The details remained obscure, but by either luck or persistence he had somehow established himself, in more than one minor dressing-room, as a dear boy. Though unable to afford supper-parties himself, for instance, he frequently made one at supper-parties given by others. Sometimes for two or three nights running he would let himself in on tiptoe, change his tails for a dressing-gown, and come straight down to breakfast.

These heady delights Nicky now clamoured to share: hatred had vanished, contempt gave place to envy. Denis was not vindictive. He took Nicky under his wing, found him a place at one or two supper-tables, and wrote the first tender note to go with his first floral offering. And he also introduced him to Lovely Leonora – Leonora Dupré – then playing at the Globe in Offenbach's 'Brigands'. She wasn't a raging, roaring, out-and-out beauty like Marie de Grey, for instance, but she was quite lovely enough, with her golden hair and eighteen-inch waist, to enslave a youthful heart. And her eyes were really fine – the true deep violet, curly-lashed, and perpetually smiling under a delicate lift of the brows. Within the first two minutes Nicky was in love; and he had never been in love before.

Passion consumed him, a passion pure and callow. He was always imagining fearful predicaments – bolting horses, blazing roofs – from which to rescue her; but in the utmost feats of daring remained quite disinterested. He wanted only to die for her. The thought of living with her never entered his head. That actresses *were* lived with he had not failed to gather; but Leonora was different. However gay and flashy on the surface – and her manners were certainly unconstrained – he knew her to be pure at heart. Nothing could shake him. Denis talked frequently of her lovers, mentioning this one and that by name: and Nicky, listening, merely pitied his simplicity. Of course she had to behave so, and be talked about so, because she was on the stage; but she didn't have lovers really; she just pretended to have them . . .

His emotions, then, were at precisely this stage when, one

night at supper, after the first performance of 'Le Petit Faust', Miss Dupré was suddenly heard to express an overwhelming desire for a small comfit-box.

'Just something small and pretty,' she kept repeating, 'to keep cachous in. An old snuff-box would do beautifully.'

As soon as he got home that night Nicky stole across the hall and into the dining-room. He dared not light the gas, but there were candle-stumps on the piano. He lit one, cautiously, and advanced to the cabinet. Yes, there it was, just as he remembered: a small blue box set round with twinkling garlands. The blue was enamel, the garlands paste: it couldn't be worth much. Nicky pulled at the glass door; it was locked, as usual, so as not to put temptation in the way of the servants. But the chessmen also were kept in the cabinet, and one wet Sunday afternoon, a long time ago, he and Bernard had made a successful experiment with the key of the writing-desk. The experiment worked still. Two minutes later, the snuff-box in his pocket, Nicky blew out the candle and stole unobtrusively upstairs.

He had never any intention of offering it in person. For one thing he was too shy, for another he felt that even the slightest suggestion of a reward – the most casual word of thanks – would rob the deed of its virtue. He was not giving a present, he was granting a wish: he wanted the box to drop as though from Heaven, unheralded, unexplained. But how to get it to her? The obvious medium of the Post Office was insufficiently romantic. So were special messengers. And at last, turning restlessly on his pillow, he thought of Cousin Denis, who had the *entrée* to her dressing-room. He could get there early one night, slip the box among her powder-puffs, and afterwards disclaim all knowledge. Only first the box must be filled, possibly with chocolate-drops, so that she should know at once what it was meant for ...

The plan now perfect in every detail, Nicky turned once more and fell asleep.

The next day was Sunday, which meant seeing Denis almost immediately: for in the late eighteen-hundreds eighteen-year-old-men-about-town still accompanied their mothers to eleven o'clock service. On the steps of St Peter's, year in, year out, Groomes and Paxtons exchanged their weekly compliments, and nothing was easier or more customary than for the boys to get separated. Under the lee of a column, church-goers streaming by on either side, Denis was hastily acquainted with his important *rôle*.

'And it ought to be done tomorrow,' added Nicky, 'or some other beast may get in first.' His desire for anonymity was perfectly genuine; but after all, it was his idea.

'You really mean it, about not letting her know?'

Nicky nodded, and under Denis's incredulous stare felt the colour mount in his cheeks. Without further parley he pulled out the snuff-box and thrust it into his cousin's hand. It was filled already, from Bernard's private store, and wrapped in a sheet of notepaper; but the paper was to be removed (did Denis understand?) before it met Leonora's eye.

Denis understood perfectly; and with clear and ingenuous foreheads they descended the steps to join their people.

The whole thing, as has been said, was completely disinterested; and this was fortunate, since in the days that followed Lovely Leonora took even less notice of Nicky than before. If anything, she paid slightly more attention to Denis. But Nicky had his consolations. He saw the snuff-box actually in her hand, he heard her describe again and again its miraculous appearance:

with secret and Jove-like mirth he sat listening in silence while she hazarded name after name. It was a pity, perhaps, that Denis could share in his emotion; but he had managed the thing too well to be grudged his reward. And, indeed, Nicky hardly cared, for the sight of Leonora's pleasure, together with his own sense of hidden power, were combining to make him a little above himself. He noted the sensation in his diary, where he described it as spiritual poise.

He had all his work cut out, however, in the days that followed, to preserve that poise intact. For the Row About the Snuff-box – so, with capitals, did it indelibly impress itself upon his youthful mind – was by common consent the Worst Row Ever. In the first place, all sorts of unexpected facts came rapidly to light. The snuff-box, in spite of being paste, was very valuable: it was worth at least fifty pounds. It was an heirloom, having belonged to Mrs Paxton's grandmother. It had been mentioned in the *Connoisseur*. It was a pity, thought young Nicky morosely, that they hadn't told him all that a lot earlier.

For there was nothing he could do. He couldn't go to Leonora and ask for it back. That was out of the question. And he couldn't tell his father, because his father inevitably *would* go to Leonora, and that – that was too awful even to think of. There was no way out, and nothing he could do save lie and suffer and probably be damned.

They questioned the servants. Cook, housemaid, parlour-maid and boy were summoned one by one into the Master's study, while Nicky, racked with sympathetic anguish, hung about in the hall. But all came out scatheless – cook red, parlour-maid white, housemaid and boot-boy both in tears. Nicky longed for Christmas to come round, so that he might tip them all heavily.

But even that was not the worst. The worst came a day later, when Mr Paxton, after apologizing in advance, required both his sons to repeat, on their honour, their first hasty disclaimers made in the heat of the discovery. For the first time since early childhood, Nicky lied to his father. He hadn't so much as noticed the thing, he said, for weeks and weeks. Then Mr Paxton apologised again, and Nicky went upstairs and wished passionately for death. Halfway up an odd thing happened: he looked so white and wan that his mother, meeting him on the landing, made a wild but brilliant guess at the truth.

'Nicky! My poor boy!'

But before she could go on, before Nicky could give himself away, Mr Paxton's great roar came bellowing from below.

'Bertha! Don't be a fool! The boy knows nothing about it!'

... So then his mother apologized to him as well, and that night at dinner, in addition to the customary sauterne, there was sherry and port. In these Bernard, with the resilience of youth, rapidly drowned all care; but Nicky was older. He was almost nineteen.

Both Mr and Mrs Paxton had a strong sense of justice, and with the first glass of sherry the Row About the Snuff-box had, as far as their household was concerned, definitely blown over. Mr Paxton indeed subsequently visited the police station, and his wife introduced spring-cleaning at least a month early: but neither police nor charwomen – naturally enough – brought anything to light. Weeks went by, the cook withdrew her notice, and little by little, save as an exciting tale at a dinner-party, the mystery of the snuff-box ceased to be mentioned. Only Nicky did not forget, much as he would have liked to; and the reason for this fidelity was a strange and distressing one.

He was, in fact, and to put it quite crudely, being unobtrusively blackmailed by his cousin Denis.

Cousin Denis knew all about the Row. He knew, from the careless lips of Bernard, even about the second questioning in Mr Paxton's study. And when, a month or two later, Nicky rather brusquely refused him a loan of five shillings, Denis idly pointed out that a fearful row could be provoked by merely mentioning the whereabouts of the snuff-box ...

'You damned little rotter!' said Nicky, in astonishment.

But he did not knock his cousin down. He lent him the five shillings.

Next time – for the tribute was not confined to cash – it was his new cane. Once it was a new bowler, swapped, under protest, against Denis's own inferior tile. Once it was a seat at the play, relinquished by Nicky on a plea of indisposition: they sent round for Denis instead, and his charmingly-expressed gratitude won Mrs Paxton's heart. Nicky listened to her praises and thought longingly of murder.

About Easter the Paxtons and Mrs Groome went for a fortnight to Lyme Regis, while Denis took himself off on a walking-tour in Wales. It lasted a week, and he and his companion, the Hon. Edward Morecombe, were both expected at Lyme for the week following. But the Honourable Edward, having twisted his ankle, put in for repairs with an aunt at Aberystwith; so that Denis had no one to check him when he boasted about his climbs. He was in high spirits, and absolutely insufferable.

To avoid seeing him, Nicky relinquished Leonora. This was easier than he had expected, for though he loved her still, she had inevitably acquired unpleasant associations. He relinquished the gay life altogether, and passed an examination or two instead. After that things got easier; for a while, at Sandhurst, rumours of her still reached him: she was engaged to an Earl, she was married to a Duke, she had a house in Maida Vale with a Turkish Entrance Hall. At Aldershot he heard less, in

India nothing at all, and during the next two or three years his tastes took their final turn from romance to polo. Lovely Leonora had not been forgotten, but she was completely out of his mind, and though for one short period in 1890 he thought of her quite often, it was only because his latest polo-pony happened to be called Leo . . .

'And a clever little beast he was!' thought the colonel.

The paper slipped from his knees, and stooping to pick it up he came back to the present. It wasn't polo ponies he had to think about, it was the snuff-box: an heirloom snuff-box, cast away by his own youthful impetuosity, and which it was now his obvious duty (assuming, of course, that Leonora hadn't lost the thing) to seek out and restore. He had no children of his own, and Bernard was dead long since; but there were Bernard's two boys, one of them recently married. 'I'll leave it to him when I die,' thought the colonel. 'People take more notice of anything that comes by will.' He looked at the paper again: on view today, sale tomorrow; but there was always the possibility, if one were prepared to pay, of a little private-treaty work beforehand. With a curious mixture of feelings – a pleasurable sadness, a faint, unaccountable excitement – Colonel Paxton walked out of the chop-house and found himself a taxi.

The house in Maida Vale was small but detached, with a rusting iron verandah and a good deal of trellis-work: a typical villa-residence, in fact, of the end of the last century. The colonel looked at it thoughtfully: when the paint was fresh and the garden full of flowers it must have been quite – what was the word? – coquettish. Quite coquettish! He advanced up the path, found the door open, and with that long-disused adjective ringing in his ear, entered Leonora's Turkish hall.

It was nothing much. A tiled floor, some daggers on the wall, and in the centre a small fountain: by such simple means as these, it seemed, had it once been possible to create a reputation. From force of habit, Colonel Paxton stepped up to a wall and took a look at the daggers. As he had suspected at the first glance, they were not Turkish at all, but inferior Soudanese.

'Wonder if she imagined the Turks took snuff?' thought the colonel; but there were no shelves or cupboards, and the low tables were bare. A couple of doorways, however, in which the doors had been replaced by bead curtains invited his attention, and rattling through the one to his right, the colonel discovered a small boudoir. (Boudoir! Another word from the past!) It was furnished, inevitably, in the style of Louis Quinze, and showed signs of recent occupation – a chair pushed back from the bureau, the bureau itself open and brimming with papers. The colonel advanced: heavy brocade curtains excluded most of the light, but he could just make out, along the mantelshelf, a row of small decorative objects. They were all china animals – cats, dogs, elephants, donkeys – such as he remembered to have seen on his aunt's window-shelf: with a snort of disgust he turned back to the desk. Its top had been cleared, and only recently, for the dust was stencilled with a variety of shapes and rings; and he was about to turn from that too when his eye was caught by one of the pigeon-holes. There was something bright in it, something that glittered . . .

For a moment the colonel paused; though the whole house was on view, that room and desk looked somehow private. Then the moment passed, and putting in his hand he drew forth the snuff-box.

It was just as he remembered it, the blue as deep, the garlands as bright: the Paxton heirloom, missing for half a century! 'I must find someone in charge,' thought the colonel, 'no need to wait for the sale'. If it were worth fifty pounds, fifty pounds he would pay; there should be no hole-and-corner chaffering over a family heirloom. Carrying the snuff-box with him – carrying it rather ostentatiously, in case anyone should think he was stealing it – Colonel Paxton recrossed the Turkish hall and looked into a small breakfast or morning-room. Here, on her knees before an open packing-case, he found exactly what he wanted – a respectable old woman in a black gown. But his precautions had been in vain: as soon as she saw the snuff-box she glared as at a thief.

'What are you doing with that box?' she asked sharply.

'I want to buy it,' explained the colonel. 'I'm looking for someone –'

'Then you're wasting your time,' cut in the old woman swiftly. 'It isn't in the sale.'

Not unreasonably nettled – for her tone was cavalier in the extreme – Colonel Paxton drew himself up in an attitude of command.

'May I ask, madam, whether you are in charge here?'

At that the woman rose, and with a long, practised, sweeping glance looked him slowly up and down.

'Yes, I am,' said she. 'I am Miss Dupré.'

For one appallingly embarrassed moment, gaping like any schoolboy, the colonel stood dumbfounded. Leonora Dupré! Lovely Leonora! The thing was impossible! But impossible or not, the woman before him was evidently in some sort of distress, and with a mighty effort he pulled himself together, closed his mouth, and opened it again to speak. Before he could find words, however, his thoughts had been read and answered.

'No, not dead yet,' said Miss Dupré wryly.

The colonel stammered.

'Don't apologize, man. Of course you thought so; everyone thought so. It's all this jumping to conclusions.' The sharp, high voice still rang with authority, biting off each word in the old professional style. 'Well, I'm not, you see. I'm selling my furniture because I happen to need some money. Fortunately I don't need much, because including yourself there have been exactly three people here.'

'If you'll sell me this snuff-box,' said the colonel boldly, 'I'll give you fifty pounds for it.'

She shook her head, but she was obviously impressed.

'I couldn't in any case,' said she, ambiguously, 'though it's a very generous offer. Wouldn't you like to see some daggers?'

'Thank you, no,' said the colonel. He looked at her narrowly: she wasn't beating up the price, she was genuinely determined not to sell. But in heaven's name, *why?* What sentimental associations could it possibly have for her? She knew nothing about it . . .

Again she read his thoughts.

'It was given me, you see –'

She broke off, and held out her hand. Scarcely knowing what he did, consumed with curiosity, Colonel Paxton put the snuff-box into it.

'It was given me,' said Miss Dupré, 'by my only true love.'

The brain of Colonel Paxton reeled, his heart thumped: tenderness, joy, above all astonishment, rocked him on his feet. For how had she known? How – in heaven's name! – was it possible that she had known? There had been no name, no message, not even a scratched initial! 'And she's known all these years!' thought the colonel fervently.

He opened his mouth, impetuous to declare himself: a flood of exquisite emotion deprived him of speech. Miss Dupré did not notice; she was lost, it seemed, in some remote and happy dream; and when at last she spoke again, her voice matched her eyes.

'He was just eighteen,' she said softly. 'Can you remember what it was like?'

The colonel nodded. Could he remember!

'I'd said one night, at supper, you see, that I wanted a little box, something old and pretty to keep cachous in. I can remember a great crowd of people, as though it was after a first night, and among the regulars one or two little boys.' Miss Dupré smiled, and for the first time in that delicate lift of the eyebrows, Lovely Leonora for a moment lived again. 'They ought to have been in bed, of course; but I never could be unkind . . . Well, the evening after, I went up to my dressing-room, and there on the table, without any name or message, was . . . *this.*'

The snuff-box winked in her palm, brilliant (thought the colonel poetically) as unshed tears in a woman's eyes. Aloud he said, shyly, ecstatically –

'The boy's –?'

'Yes. The boy's. He hadn't wanted me to know.' Miss Dupré smiled again, tenderly as a mother. 'But the accident happened, and I did know, and – and I still keep his photograph. Look!'

Under the long, still-manicured fingers the box flew open. Completely overcome, rocking anew with joy and bewilderment, Colonel Paxton bent over her hand and saw pasted inside the lid a small, much-faded snapshot of his cousin Denis Groome.

A long way off, Miss Dupré was still speaking.

'I think it was the only time in my life I'd ever been early; and there he was, pink as a paeony, just slipping it among my face-creams. How he got up I can't think; he must have bribed the doorman with a week's pocket-money. And there was no name, no message, nothing to show who it came from; if I hadn't caught him I should never have known. He didn't mean me to know, you see, he didn't want even my thanks. He was so sweet that I think I cried.'

'My God!' ejaculated the colonel.

She looked at him kindly, as at one who understood and felt for her.

'It does one good to cry sometimes. It makes you feel younger. But afterwards, when we were laughing again, I realized that I oughtn't to let him give it me; it was too valuable. I tried to make him take it back, only he wouldn't. We wrangled for days, until at last I got him to promise me that if ever he were hard up he'd send that minute and ask for it back. After that I didn't mind; I used to show it all round and pretend to wonder where it came from.' Miss Dupré smiled. 'We still kept up the secret, you see. I don't quite know why; I suppose anything seems funny when you're really in love.'

With an odd, stiff gesture, as though he were trying to stop something, the colonel put up his hand. But she did not see him; she was looking at the snuff-box.

'And it was real, with Denis and me. I ought to know; I've seen enough of the other. But he was so young and sweet, and he didn't want anything –' The snuff-box turned slowly in her hand. 'That was to begin with, of course; afterwards, he did – want.'

She broke off, eyebrows a little tilted, and looked directly up as though to meet the colonel's judgment.

'At first I thought I oughtn't to,' she said, simply, 'because he was such a kid and might get into trouble over it. But then he got worse and worse, and I worried over him like a hen with one chick. But it wasn't worrying would do him any good. I don't think anyone could have blamed me really, not even his mother . . .'

With a great effort the colonel said stupidly, 'So you did, then? I mean, you *did*?'

'Yes. I can't think why I'm telling you, except that it's all so long ago. No secrets matter after half a century. We went to Paris, just for a week, and – you'll never believe it! – it was the first time I'd ever been there. I'd always pretended I had, of course, like all the others.'

She broke off again, she waited for him to say something; but the colonel had no words. '*That Welsh walking tour*,' he was thinking. '*That Welsh walking tour with the boy who damaged his leg!*' And then he thought, 'But I can't tell her. How can I tell her? She's been thinking of this thing for years. She's got it all pat . . .'

'I understand,' he muttered at last. 'You want to keep it as – as a memento.'

She smiled.

'No. Not quite that, either. You remember what I made him promise, if he should ever need the money? Well, yesterday he wrote,' said Miss Dupré simply.

For perhaps twenty seconds the words beat meaninglessly on the colonel's ear; then the full force of the dilemma rushed in and overwhelmed him. It was fantastic! There his snuff-box lay – his heirloom family snuff-box – not a couple of feet away from him; and the instant his back was turned she was going to send it to old Groome! To old Groome – good God! – who had already used it once as a means of blackmail, and once as a means to a mistress! This time, no doubt, he meant to sell it outright; he was always wanting money. The thing was fantastic, it was impossible; and yet the only way to stop it – by telling the woman the truth, by repeating and proving till she at last believed – that was impossible, too. Her one true love, she had said: you couldn't destroy a thing like that ... 'After all,' thought the colonel, 'I can always get it out of old Groome afterwards ...'

'So now you understand,' she was saying, 'why I can't sell it to you. Even if he hadn't sent for it.'

Colonel Paxton bowed.

'But you mustn't think I'm sorry to be parting with it. I'm glad – glad he still remembered after all these years. If I've been crying a little that's just my temperament.' She held out her hand; with a sincere impulse of admiration, the colonel raised it to his lips. 'And – I thank you for listening to me,' said Leonora Dupré.

Instead of taking another taxi the colonel returned by tube. He genuinely feared lest, in the solitude of a cab, he might be seized by an apoplexy. The company of fellow-creatures made control easier; for no man more than the colonel abhorred scenes in public. Teeth gritted under his moustache, he sat outwardly calm all the way from Maida Vale to Piccadilly Circus. He had only one desire – or rather one desire embracing a complicated series of actions. He wanted to take old Groome by the collar, kick him down the steps of the club, horsewhip him in St James's Street, denounce him at length in the presence of his peers, and finally sit over him with a pistol till the arrival of the post. So boiled and swelled the colonel's wrath; but under those surges ached a deeper hurt still. He had been robbed not only of a snuff-box – not only of rightful credit and a new bowler – but also of a lovely and innocent dream. He did not put it in those words, of course; he only knew that he had suffered, during the last half-hour, an irreparable loss.

'I'll never speak to him again,' thought the colonel.

The club was reached; and there, in profile against the window, sat Denis Groome waiting for his game of chess.

'No more chess for *him*,' thought the colonel viciously.

And for the first time in years, standing there on the pavement, he regarded his cousin with attention. Thin, silvery hair, mummified hands, skin like badly-stretched parchment: neither dead nor alive he looked, but just – what was it? – just lasting out.

'The poor old buffer!' thought Colonel Paxton.

The desire to horsewhip was rapidly leaving him. A fellow with one foot in the grave – there wouldn't be any satisfaction. And as for publishing his shame, what would old Groome care for that? Who, apart from the colonel himself, would be in the least interested by it? He hadn't a friend in the world, barely an acquaintance: treated everyone like dirt and refused to learn Contract. Some years ago, when it first came in, the colonel offered to teach him out of a handbook; and old Groome had declined, saying it was obviously no game for gentlemen. Well, now there was no more chess (thought Colonel Paxton) perhaps he'd regret it . . .

And then, suddenly, like a bolt from the blue, another thought occurred to him. It was new, disconcerting, yet dreadfully relevant.

There would – if old Groome were properly punished – there would, in that case, be no more chess for himself either.

'If I don't speak to old Groome,' thought the colonel, 'who on earth *shall* I speak to?'

The accuracy of the phrase startled him. On the whole face of the earth, who else was there left? Bernard's two boys, of course – but they didn't want him. And even if they did, he couldn't see himself very often in their potty little suburban hutches. As for the others – men he'd known in the regiment, men he nodded to at the club – he could barely remember their faces, let alone their names. Denis Groome, the damned old scoundrel, was at least somebody one *knew* . . .

And what good would be done after all? Bernard's boy would get the snuff-box, the colonel's anger would be properly assuaged. Only it was assuaged already, the emotion troubling him now was not wrath, but an overwhelming melancholy. It was nostalgia, it was the pathos of old age. Above all, it was the fear of loneliness.

'Supposing,' thought the colonel, guiltily, 'supposing I let him keep the damn' thing?'

Suddenly conscious of fatigue, he turned and went up the steps. In the club vestibule, directly opposite the door, was an ancient silvery mirror: it reflected a little old gentleman, still passably erect, but inclining to jerkiness. The colonel crossed it quickly and went on into the reading-room.

'You're late,' said old Groome, lowering his paper.

The colonel looked at him heavily.

'Yes,' he said, 'I'm late. I've been detained.' And drawing up to the chess-board, he opened as usual with a Ruy Lopez.

Seal Tregarthen's Cousin

THE ISLAND WAS off the coast of Cornwall, the smallest and most outlying of a small group three hours from the mainland; and all through the spring, autumn and winter its inhabitants, who lived by fishing and flower-growing, numbered exactly a dozen. But in summer this number was augmented, by the arrival of the Cattletts, to fourteen. On every first of August Mr and Mrs Cattlett set out from their home in Chelsea to make the tedious journey by train, steamer and row-boat; and on every second, as he stepped ashore, George Cattlett said the same thing.

'Back,' said George Cattlett, 'to Nature!'

There was no doubt that the island was very natural indeed. Apart from the one narrow strip of flower gardens it was completely uncultivated. Its weather-beaten rocks, its cliffs cushioned with sea-pinks, knew not the hand of man. The jetty was little more than a tongue of loose stones and a rough wall. The cottage occupied by the Cattletts – like all the rest – had outdoor sanitation only. But the Cattletts did not care, they were simple-lifers of the old school, and but for the exigencies of George Cattlett's position as art master at a girls' college would willingly have lived on their island all the year round.

They always thought and spoke of it as theirs, for as George Cattlett so rightly said, Appreciation is Ownership; and it often seemed to them that its actual inhabitants hardly appreciated the island at all. They were always too busy fishing or planting bulbs, and when they had nothing to do had the curious habit of going inside their houses to do it. Maud Cattlett, who took a great interest in arts and crafts, once tried to interest them in weaving, but with a complete lack of success. That was on her first visit, and though she carried down her handloom again the year after, the year after that she left it at home. In time she discarded also her wood-carving implements and her spinning-wheel, and the Cattletts were able to make the journey encumbered only by one suitcase, two easels, and their personal supply of canvases, brushes and paints.

'Back,' said George Cattlett, 'to Nature!'

At the end of the jetty, awaiting them, stood Seal Tregarthen. As the keel of the row-boat grated on the pebbles he stooped down, with one hand grasped the bows, with the other helped Mrs Cattlett ashore. George Cattlett, disdaining assistance, leapt lightly out into four inches of water, but only laughed at the mishap. As his wife often said, the island turned him into a perfect schoolboy.

'Home again!' said George gaily.

Seal Tregarthen nodded. He was a heavy giant of a man, too blond and big-boned for the true island type, of which his beautiful wife was the dark and perfect flower. Mary Tregarthen stood a little behind her husband, smiling gravely. Her presence gave the landing a touch of ceremony; always she came down with Seal to greet the Cattletts, to conduct them up to their tiny cottage, and to make them a cup of tea; and the Cattletts were always sorry to see her go, since this was almost their only social contact with island life. She spoke briefly of the weather and the flower-crop, waited until her husband had carried up the baggage – all under one gigantic arm – and courteously took her leave.

'I sometimes wonder,' said Mrs Cattlett suddenly, 'whether they really *like* us.'

'Of course they do,' said George, 'They simply aren't demonstrative. They're too close to the soil.'

'I know, George. That's why I'm so fond of them. But – it does seem so hard to win their confidence. You go fishing with Seal, for instance, but you never bring back any . . . gossip.'

The word was misplaced, and she knew it. George frowned.

'Gossip? Thank God there isn't any. You painted Mrs Tregarthen's portrait . . .'

'I tried to,' said Maud, with genuine humility.

'. . . and you didn't get any gossip out of *her*. If you wanted gossip, we should have gone to Bournemouth.'

'I didn't,' said Maud, more humbly still. 'Come and look out of the window, dear . . .'

As always the sight of so much sea at once restored peace. For some minutes the Cattletts stood side by side, breathing deep breaths as they had been taught to do in a course on Physical Culture. Then they turned to their unpacking, and as soon as it was finished walked down towards the quay.

They passed a row of three cottages, housing respectively three Penruddocks, two Jasper Penruddocks, and three Ambroses. A little farther on came the cottage of the Tregarthens, and down by the shore the cottage of the two Ambrose cousins. The whole population of the island was concentrated in that one hamlet, but not a soul could be seen. The day's work was done, all were within doors. Only as the Cattletts passed each window, a curtain flickered.

Peacefully, monotonously, the days slipped by. The Cattletts set up their easels, George before a pool in the rock, Maud before the easier outline of a cliff, and worked with diligence.

Their talents were worse than mediocre, but they had a lot of fun. George also watched seabirds through his field-glasses, and went trawling for pollock with Seal Tregarthen. On one occasion he stayed out all night. He did not feel very well next day, and Maud had to clean his jacket with turpentine. In the evenings they played bézique and backgammon, or George read aloud to his wife. In this way all of August passed, and the first week in September; and then one day, as she strolled alone towards the jetty, Maud Cattlett received the surprise of her life.

Leaning against the extreme point of the wall was a stranger. He was neither a Penruddock nor an Ambrose. He was also the biggest man Mrs Cattlett had ever seen. He was bigger even than Seal Tregarthen: he was monumental. His shoulders were like the shoulders of an Atlas, his legs, clad in rust-coloured trousers, were like twin pillars. It seemed marvellous that the wall could support his weight.

A long shadow fell between Mrs Cattlett and the sun. She turned round and saw Seal Tregarthen.

'Who,' gasped Mrs Cattlett, 'is that?'

Seal Tregarthen, as usual, took his time about answering. He looked at the leaning figure, and looked at Mrs Cattlett, and finally looked at the sea.

'Cousin,' he said at last.

'When did he get here?'

'Last night.'

'But how—'

'Off a fisherman,' said Tregarthen. He shifted his gaze from the ocean to Mrs Cattlett, and with an obvious effort gave the next piece of information unasked. 'Come back to lend me a hand,' said Tregarthen. 'If Mr Cattlett wants any fishing, say I'll be out tonight.'

Thus dismissed, Maud hurried back to find her husband, whom she had left sitting on his favourite rock at an angle of the path. It was not often that the island provided such a piece of news; to a community of a dozen persons the addition even of one was highly important. Mrs Cattlett arrived at the rock so obviously excited that George sprang up to meet her.

'What is it, Maud?' he cried. 'Has anything happened?'

Mrs Cattlett nodded violently.

'Look George! Look on the end of the jetty!'

George unslung his glasses and focused them. His reactions were all that could be desired.

'Good heavens!' he exclaimed. 'What a terrific fellow! Who is he?'

'Seal Tregarthen's cousin,' said Mrs Cattlett proudly.

'How did he get here?'

'Off one of the fishing boats, last night. He's come to lend Seal a hand. Look, dear – he's making this way!'

Moved by a quite disproportionate interest the Cattletts stood to watch. With very long, very slow strides Seal Tregarthen's cousin walked the length of the jetty, nodded to Tregarthen, and disappeared behind the angle of the wall. A moment later his head and shoulders were again visible, moving steadily above the hedge as he mounted the cliff path; presently only a dozen yards and a corner separated him from the Cattletts' seat. His advance seemed as slow and as irresistible as the advance of the tide; and suddenly, as the waters over-run the last inches of sand, he was upon them – bigger than both the Cattletts put together.

'Good morning,' said George. 'You're Seal Tregarthen's cousin?'

The man nodded. He did not exactly stop, but he slowed his long stride and swayed towards them. His big head was thatched with tow-coloured hair, his face was deeply tanned, and as his long-sighted blue eyes rested on her husband's face Mrs Cattlett had a sudden vision of a cart-horse leaning bene-volently over a sparrow. She put the thought from her at once; but it was strange how Seal Tregarthen's cousin always suggested, right from the start, analogies with the cruder forms of Nature.

'It's a fine day,' said Mr Cattlett.

Seal Tregarthen's cousin nodded again, and the rhythm of his stride carried him past the rock. But the Cattletts were left with no sense of having been treated discourteously; they rather felt pleased with themselves, as though they had been noticed by someone in a procession. They also felt the slight blankness that comes after a procession has passed.

'There, now!' exclaimed George Cattlett. 'We never found out his name!'

They never did. To them, as (it seemed) to everyone else on the island, the newcomer remained Seal Tregarthen's Cousin. He slipped easily and naturally into the island life, fished with Tregarthen, worked in Tregarthen's garden, and lodged in the Tregarthen cottage. Maud Cattlett, her feminine curiosity scenting a feminine ally, took a half-knitted sock and went down to ask the beautiful Mrs Tregarthen how one turned heels – after which it was only natural to comment on the new arrival; but Mrs Tregarthen's manners were equalled only by her discretion.

'Your visitor looks like a strong man?' hazarded Maud.

Mary Tregarthen nodded. This universal taciturnity was one of the local characteristics the Cattletts most prized – 'Our dear silent island!' as they used to say to each other – but there were times when it could be irritating. Maud tried again.

'Do you know, I don't think we know his name?'

'He's my husband's cousin,' said Mary, raising her dark eyes in a steady gaze. 'Watch now, Mrs Cattlett, while I start the narrowing . . .'

Maud obediently watched. That was another thing about the islanders: they had the faculty of making themselves obeyed. Mrs Cattlett learnt how to turn a heel, if she learnt nothing about Seal Tregarthen's Cousin.

'He's like a Force of Nature,' she told her husband admiringly; and made several attempts to paint his portrait – but only from memory, since there was something about him which made her reluctant to ask for sittings. Not that he was in the least fierce, or rough; on the contrary, his manners were marked by their gentleness, he did everything very quietly, and never raised his voice; but Mrs Cattlett felt that to sit opposite him, in silence, for hours on end, would be too much. She felt she might become hypnotized, as one can become hypnotized from gazing too long upon the sea or upon a high hill. She did not mention this idea to George, but she noticed that Mr Cattlett himself, after each of his fishing trips with the cousins, was always unusually ready for a game of backgammon, or a hand of bézique, or some other bright domestic employment.

A week of pleasant days passed; never, as the Cattletts told each other, had they felt nearer to Mother Nature. Mrs Cattlett worked at her portrait, Mr Cattlett fished for pollock and worked at his pool; and then came Saturday and the weekly bunch of papers from the mainland.

Apart from the headlines, the Cattletts always read the art criticism first, then the literary supplements, then the dramatic notices, then any items about the Royal family; so that it was often several days before they got round to the body of the news. George, on this occasion, got round first: by Tuesday night he had reached a quite obscure paragraph dealing with a rowdy episode in a French café. The name of the café was Le Coq Rouge; it was situated on the water-front at St. Malo, and the facts were simple.

On the night of the fifth a Frenchman, known only by his soubriquet of Le Petit Danilo, had in the course of an argument struck his woman companion across the mouth; whereupon an anonymous Englishman lifted him from his seat and threw him out on to the quay. On the cobblestones of the quay Le Petit Danilo was found with a broken neck; the Englishman had not been found at all, and it was believed that he had made good his escape in one of several fishing-boats then putting out. He was variously described as a sailor and as a fisherman; but all witnesses agreed that he was blue-eyed, fair-headed, and of gigantic size.

'Maud,' said George Cattlett. 'Read that . . .'

Maud read; then she too sat staring at the paper.

'The fifth,' pointed out Mr Cattlett. 'The day you saw him was the seventh, and he'd been landed the night before. From St. Malo to here by fishing-boat would take just about twenty-four hours.'

There was no need to explain whom he meant; the gigantic figure of Seal Tregarthen's Cousin was present in both their minds.

'And he was wearing French trousers,' went on George unhappily. 'Those tan-coloured canvas ones. We've seen them on the French fishermen at Penrythen. He isn't wearing them any more.'

Mrs Cattlett folded the paper and placed it carefully in her paint-box. She was deeply troubled.

'You really think . . .?'

'Don't you?'

'Whatever I think,' said Maud, 'I don't see that it's our business. His description will be circulated. The police must have it already.'

'The police!' repeated George grimly. 'The police don't come *here*!'

This was true. There were police at Penrythen, on the mainland, there was one solitary constable on the largest of the islands, but in practice the islanders lived outside the pale of the Law. They were noticeably casual about such things as gun and dog-licences, if they were no longer wreckers they were certainly smugglers; their attitude to their own policeman was one of live and let live. If he didn't trouble them, they wouldn't trouble him; and since their instincts were sporting rather than criminal, the system worked very well. It was not, however, a system designed to co-operate with international law.

'It's a question of duty,' said George. 'A man has been killed . . .'

'I know, dear. That's terrible. And yet, to set the police on anyone – that seems so terrible too. After all, we aren't *sure*.'

George looked at her and her eyes fell. Quite apart from the physical description, the whole story fitted. It was so exactly what Seal Tregarthen's Cousin would do: no word, no reproof, simply the contemptuous removal of an offensive object. That death had followed was the merest accident . . .

'It wouldn't be murder,' said George. 'It would be man-slaughter at the most.

'Let's think it over!' pleaded Maud. 'A day or two more won't matter. After all, he's here, under our eye!'

That was the trouble. Seal Tregarthen's Cousin was there, under their eye. He moved about them, tranquil, stately and benevolent, like the presiding deity of the island. He never spoke much, but all his words were grave and kindly; and the two Penruddock children followed him like puppies.

'I can't help it,' said Maud. 'Whatever he's done, it would be so dreadful to shut him up. It would be wrong.'

'I wish I knew what to do,' said George.

In the end they did nothing. The soft island air, the quiet routine of the island life, seemed to lull their civic instincts. They let day after day slip by, and presently the whole matter seemed to lose importance. After all, it was only an accident. Whoever killed him, the Frenchman had obviously deserved to die. Whoever killed him . . .

At the end of September the Cattletts returned to Chelsea and were at once caught up in their other life. They were very busy; George had his teaching, Maud had the flat to run, and in addition they belonged to innumerable societies for the spreading of culture and the betterment of the world. Their minds were so fully occupied that gradually all holiday memories faded altogether; until one night George brought home a fellow-artist who had just returned from France.

He had returned, to be more exact, from St Malo.

It was Maud who asked the first question. She couldn't help herself.

'Did you hear anything of a – a disturbance there last summer, at a café called Le Coq Rouge?'

'When Le Petit Danilo was thrown out on his neck and killed? Certainly,' said the artist. He smiled, pleased to display his familiarity with water-front life. 'They talk about it still. Where did you hear of it?'

'My wife read a paragraph in the paper,' said George uneasily.

'It made headlines at St Malo. The Englishman seems to have been the biggest chap ever seen. *Un géant blond . . .*'

'Did they ever,' asked Maud, 'catch him?'

The artist shook his head.

'They didn't, and they won't. There were three fishing-boats putting out just as it all happened, and he could have tumbled straight off the quay into any one of them. The police got hold of the skippers later, of course, and collected a lobster apiece, but no information. The sailormen weren't talking.'

'Have some more coffee,' said George.

The next day, as though to occupy their minds still further, he put down his own and his wife's name for yet another course of lectures, this time on Citizenship.

It was the most unfortunate thing he could have done. Every other Wednesday night through April, May and June the Cattletts sat in a church hall and were exhaustively instructed in their civic duties; with the result that after the last lecture George Cattlett came home and drank three whiskies-and-sodas in quick succession. He had never done such a thing before, and Maud watched him with alarm.

'It's killing me!' exploded George. 'I have thought and thought! I have been thinking day and night about Seal Tregarthen's Cousin!'

Maud's face grew troubled. She could guess what was coming.

'I have failed in my duty,' continued George wretchedly. 'Out there, on the island, it all seemed different. I don't know what happened to me. I don't know why I didn't go straight to the authorities at once. Because if the man is guilty he must be punished, and if he is innocent, no harm will have been done.'

'Yes, it will,' said Maud quickly. 'Even if they don't take him away and lock him up there'll be police and detectives and – and journalists, George, writing up our island, turning it into a murder-mystery, spoiling and vulgarizing it all . . .'

'Stop!' cried George.

He sat in silent misery, his head in his hands, a conscientious beauty-lover torn between two ideals. It was only the whisky, as Maud firmly believed, which that night saved his reason by overpowering it. When she spoke to him again it was apparent that he was three-parts unconscious.

'I must think,' he muttered, as Maud tenderly helped him to bed. 'I must go on thinking . . .'

For another month the struggle continued. Neither of them mentioned the subject again, but it was continually present in their minds. On the first of August Maud, half-fearfully, packed as usual the easels and the suitcases and the boxes of paints. George made no demur. They caught their usual train from Paddington; and then it was, during that sleepless night – passed sitting up in a third-class carriage – that the long dilemma at last resolved itself. Physical discomfort no doubt had its effect: they were too tired to struggle any more. When they got out in the morning on to Penrythen platform they knew, without exchanging a word, that the die was cast. George's mind was made up; and Maud had submitted.

'We may as well deposit the baggage,' said George.

Maud nodded dumbly. She knew what he meant; they had to tell, but they could never go back to their island afterwards. They would have to seek out some other, some inferior spot.

With hearts heavy but resolved they turned their steps towards the police station. At its portal Mrs Cattlett drew back for the last time.

'George,' she whispered, 'there won't be a reward?'

'I shouldn't think so,' said George; 'if there is, of course we shan't take it.'

'They couldn't *make* us?'

'Of course not,' said George.

A little assuaged, Maud followed him into the presence of the Sergeant. The Sergeant was small and sandy, and not in the least imposing; but he represented the Law. When he asked what he could do for them both the Cattletts instinctively displayed all the signs of guilt.

'There's a man,' began George distractedly, 'out on an island there, called Seal Tregarthen's Cousin.'

The Sergeant looked at him with interest.

'Seal Tregarthen's Cousin?'

'Yes,' said George. 'And I think you ought to know . . .'

'He's dead,' said the Sergeant.

The Cattletts stared stupidly.

'Drowned,' said the Sergeant.

'Drowned,' repeated George. 'Dead? But that's – that's incredible. I beg your pardon, but are you sure?'

'I'm afraid so, sir. The body was identified by all his folk on the island. He was lost with his boat, and washed ashore.'

'But – when?'

'Matter of four months back. We lost a ketch from here at the same time. It's a cruel coast in a storm.'

'I still can't believe it,' said Maud. 'I mean – he wasn't the sort of man to die . . .'

The Sergeant did not laugh.

'Proper big chap, wasn't he? That's what the coastguard said: a proper Hercules. What was it you wanted him for?'

Between the Cattletts passed a quick glance. Then George cleared his throat nervously. He wasn't used to lying.

'As a matter of fact, it was simply that he – er – owed me a small debt. But it's of no account, now.'

The Sergeant nodded sympathetically; and the Cattletts went out.

They could still go back to their island. At least it wasn't spoilt. Tragedy had touched it, but not squalor. They retrieved their baggage, and boarded the steamer as usual, and on reaching the largest of the islands transferred themselves as usual to their accustomed row-boat. Everything was the same – the salt of the sea, the softness of the air, the sudden quietness, that always marked this last stage of their journey. Everything was the same, until they reached the island.

At the end of the jetty, awaiting them, stood Seal Tregarthen's Cousin.

As the keel of the boat grated on the pebbles he stooped down, with one hand grasped the bows, with the other assisted Mrs Cattlett ashore. Or such was his intention; but Maud, uttering a loud dry, dropped down again into the arms of the boatman. The craft rocked violently; George Cattlett jumped, landed in the water, and stood there transfixed, the wavelets lapping round his ankles.

'Mr Cattlett, you'll be sopped,' said Mary Tregarthen.

She had been standing a little way up the jetty, the usual grave smile of welcome on her lips; now she advanced, ready to receive Maud Cattlett as the boatman thrust her out. Sheer force of habit enabled George to pay the man his fee; then the boat was run out again, and the sound of its oars diminished over the water.

'But you're drowned!' cried Mrs Cattlett violently.

Seal Tregarthen's Cousin slowly shook his big head.

'That was my cousin,' he said.

'But we asked at Penrythen!' cried Maud. 'We said "Seal Tregarthen's Cousin" – and they told us he was dead!'

The big head nodded.

'That's right: my cousin. *I'm* Seal Tregarthen.'

Maud turned almost wildly to the woman.

'Seal Tregarthen . . .'

'This is Seal,' said Mary steadily. 'They were cousins, Mrs Cattlett, and they had the same name. Like the Ambroses and the Jasper Penruddocks: we've all the same names around here.'

'Then it's your husband,' said Maud, pity struggling with bewilderment, 'your husband who has been drowned? I'm so sorry . . .'

'He went as he'd wished,' said Mary Tregarthen. The words were like an epitaph. She lifted her head and looked up at the giant beside her. 'Seal's my man now, Mrs Cattlett; we're to wed soon as we can come at a parson.'

Maud's mouth opened and shut. There are, as a rule, no phrases which come more readily to the tongue than those of congratulation; but this was a case to which the rules did not apply.

Mary smiled.

'We're not blood-kin, Mrs Cattlett,' she said kindly, 'and a woman can't abide here alone.'

She went up with them to their cottage, and made them a cup of tea, and spoke of the fishing and the flower-harvest, and then left them to their startled thoughts.

'I can understand,' said George Cattlett at last. 'I can understand in a way. When Seal turned up there was a Seal Tregarthen here before him; so he was Seal Tregarthen's Cousin. And when Seal Tregarthen was drowned he – the cousin – came into his name again. And the man who was drowned *was* Seal Tregarthen's Cousin . . . I admit it's confusing.'

'And yet in another way,' said Maud thoughtfully, 'it's so simple. So natural. You can see how his mind worked. And the minds – I suppose – of everyone on the island. When the coastguards, the policeman, came to investigate and asked who the man was, they just said Seal Tregarthen's Cousin.'

'And he was. In a way,' said George, 'he undoubtedly was.' He took a turn or two round the room, and came back to his wife. 'What troubles me, Maud, is this: Seal Tregarthen's Cousin – the man *we* knew as Seal's Cousin – had, I am more and more convinced, every reason to change his identity. And he *has* changed his identity. As you say, he's done it in the simplest, most natural way possible. And I ask myself, *was* it so – so unconscious after all? Was it the act of a child of Nature, or the act of a clever criminal?'

'George!'

'And *then* I ask myself,' continued George, 'are we still justified in letting the matter rest?'

The words were firm enough, but the tone was not. Already George Cattlett's neat and conscientious spirit recoiled before the inevitable complications of a putative charge against a potentially dead man. The whole island, without a doubt, would swear to Seal Tregarthen's identity. The islanders might be cunning, or they might be simple-minded, but without doubt they were loyal. Also, they didn't want trouble . . .

'Look, George,' said Maud gently. 'Look out of the window.'

Seal Tregarthen was coming up the path. Slowly, steadily, he mounted towards them, their baggage packed easily under one arm. The evening light magnified his figure, his shadow stretched gigantic; on his huge face was an expression of profound peace. Either he had no crime on his conscience, or he had no conscience. The Cattletts were never to know which.

'Of course we're justified,' whispered Maud, 'because we can't do anything else. He's too much for us, George; we can't cope with him. No one could: not with a Force of Nature . . .'

Driving Home

HENRY CHEVRON was driving home to London after a day in the country, when he remembered that he had promised to bring his wife a dozen fresh eggs. He was an architect, and the trip had been one of business, not pleasure – to advise on the conversion of a stately home into a country club; but his client had provided an excellent lunch, and this made Henry all the more anxious to procure Catherine her eggs. For half the ten years of their marriage they had been a very attached couple, and now that their attachment was worn away they clung all the more, in all their dealings with each other, to this sort of playing fair.

Henry dropped to twenty. He wasn't on any popular route where a stall might neighbour a filling-station, but in the next village a crudely-lettered sign caught his eye, FRESH PRO-DUCE; so he stopped outside the small brick cottage and sounded his horn. After a few moments a young woman emerged and looked at him impatiently.

'Eggs?' asked Henry.

'Sorry, we haven't got none,' snapped the young woman.

Henry asked if she knew where he might be luckier.

'Well, you could try Mrs Cox. She's at the other end,' said the young woman. 'If you'll 'scuse me, we're watching the telly.'

She turned and immediately went in again. Henry leaned on his horn and shouted for further directions. Of what the young woman called over her shoulder he distinguished only one word, and that an odd one. It sounded like 'witch'. From a patron of television this seemed unlikely; Henry shrugged and drove on – but slowly, in case Mrs Cox, witch or no, had a sign out saying Eggs.

At the end of the little street he in fact found what he was looking for – not an egg sign, indeed, but a dwelling slightly larger than the rest with the name Wychwood Cot fading from its gate. Henry grinned to himself, stopped again, and got out.

No one answered his ring, but he knew enough of country ways to go round to the back and try there. The garden behind was a mere strip of rough grass terminated by a tall, gappy hedge with apple-trees showing above; more importantly, about this apology for a lawn strayed several hens. Henry knocked at the back door and waited.

Again, no one answered. He stepped back a pace or two and looked up for a television aerial. It was there all right, and no doubt Mrs Cox was there too inside, glued to her set. To put his head through the door and call out seemed the only plan; the knob turning easily under his hand, Henry tentatively entered – and at the same moment was himself transfixed by a screech from the rear. Up from the apple-orchard an old, old woman came running and screeching her head off.

'What do you want? Who are you? What do you want in my house?' she screamed out.

Henry waited until she was beside him, and moderately explained his errand.

'I can't hear you, I'm deaf!' shouted the woman – and with a strong old hand on his wrist held him firmly where he was. He wouldn't have been surprised if she'd blown a police-whistle. 'Who are you?' she repeated furiously. 'What's your name?'

There was no reason why Henry should tell her, but he did. It seemed, at the moment, impossible not to. Of course she couldn't hear. She pulled him in, into some sort of scullery, and indicated on the draining-board a paper bag. There was already something scrawled across it: '*No bottles out,*' read Henry, '*so I left none. The Milkman.*'

The woman pushed a pencil into his hand. 'Go on, write who you are!' she ordered; and Henry obediently wrote his name below – adding the query, 'Eggs?' 'Never heard of you!' she shouted. 'Don't sell eggs! Go away, go away, go away!'

Henry was only too glad to. Actually, a hundred yards farther on he came to a gate lettered Wychwood Farm, and there bought his dozen fresh eggs without the least difficulty. It slightly disturbed him, he didn't know why, that he'd left his name with Mrs Cox. (Who, presumably, wasn't Mrs Cox at all.) He didn't know why, but he wished he hadn't; and to forget the episode all the sooner, said nothing about it to his wife.

He got in about eight, and they dined together as usual in the restaurant attached to the big modern block of flats. Their apartment included a kitchenette, and in the first years of their marriage they often dined there – Catherine cooking while Henry looked on, then both of them washing up to sugary music on the radio; but the habit had lapsed along with many others, and now Catherine used the kitchen only to cook herself a luncheon omelette. It was simpler to eat in the restaurant, also a little conversation with neighbouring diners covered any silence between themselves.

'I shouldn't mind an early night,' said Henry, as they finished. 'I'm rather tired.'

Catherine didn't enquire into his day's events; if she had, he might have enquired into hers; as it was, he didn't notice the omission.

It was in the next day's evening paper that he saw the paragraph with his own name in it.

Otherwise he mightn't have noticed it at all. It was quite a short paragraph: the old woman of Wychwood Cot, even coshed and robbed, rated no more in the London press. But one's eye notoriously picks out, from any page of print, one's own name; and beneath the headline, MOTORIST MAY AID POLICE, an obviously official release expressed Scotland Yard's desire to interview a Mr Henry Chevron. In connection (Henry read on) with an attack the previous evening upon Mrs Selina Louisa Parkin, seventy, of Wychwood Cot, Skrimbles, Oxfordshire.

Absurdly enough, Henry's first thought was that he'd been right about her not being Mrs Cox. She wasn't: she was Mrs Parkin.

Of course he put the frivolous point aside at once. He wasn't exactly worried, but he saw the need to clear things up as soon as possible. Actually when he read the paragraph he was already on his way home, by Underground, from his office, and there seemed no point in getting out to telephone when he could do so ten minutes later from his own flat. His decision to contact the police was instant, and solid – their investigation of himself being obviously pure routine, necessary if tiresome, and the sooner dealt with the better. Henry Chevron was both a sensible man and a good citizen. He returned to the paragraph with calm, and from it learned that Mrs Parkin had been struck about the head with a blunt instrument, and discovered, still unconscious, still clutching an empty handbag, next morning by the milkman. 'I suppose no bottles out again,' said Henry aloud. His neighbour looked at him curiously; sensible, good citizen as he was, Henry Chevron felt glad to be anonymous. He offered the neighbour an ingratiating smile – and immediately asked himself why. 'It's more of a shock than one realizes,' thought Henry – sensibly. 'I'll telephone as soon as I get in . . .'

As it was, he had no need to. The police were there before him.

What was he? – the extremely well-mannered, youngish-middle-aged, broad-shouldered, shrewd-eyed visitor? Detective-Superintendent, detective-sergeant, higher in rank or lower? Henry and Catherine never knew. He told them, but they could never remember. To them he was simply the Police; also the Law.

'You've been quick,' said Henry Chevron.

It wasn't what he'd have said if he'd thought. But he hadn't time to think. Letting himself in with his latch-key, making straight for the telephone in the sitting-room, he hadn't thought even what he'd say to Catherine . . .

The policeman smiled modestly.

'It's an unusual name, sir. Chevron is a very unusual name.'

'I was just going to telephone you,' said Henry. 'I only read about it on my way home; I was just going to telephone you.'

'Why do you both say everything twice over?' asked Catherine irritably. 'Won't it all take twice as long?'

Henry glanced across at her. She was irritated, possibly nervous; but some marital sixth sense told him she didn't yet know what it was all about.

'Hasn't he told you?' asked Henry – in marital shorthand.

'I've only just got here,' interposed the policeman mildly.

'I've only just come in myself,' said Catherine. 'He was waiting outside. He just asked –'

'You haven't seen an evening paper?'

She shook her head.

'Then you'd better know,' said Henry, 'that an old woman I tried to buy eggs off, last night, has been hit over the head. Hence the investigation – initiated, as I remarked before, with commendable speed.'

Surprisingly, it was the policeman who thrust a hand under Catherine's elbow. Henry simply felt all his wife's irritation transferred to himself. There was, after all, nothing to faint about . . .

'If I may say so, sir, a little sudden,' rebuked the policeman – carefully assisting Catherine to the sofa. But it seemed he wasn't really cross with Henry either; again he smiled his modest smile. 'As for speed, I only wish all our jobs were so easy. You left, as you might say, your card; and at Wychwood Farm, where you bought eggs – you did buy eggs there, sir?'

'Certainly,' agreed Henry. 'One dozen fresh.'

' – there they fancied you heading for London. So it was really very simple, you being the only Chevron in the directory. And now, sir, if you care to tell me anything you know of Mrs Parkin, describe your visit to her and so on, besides helping us get the picture, we mayn't need to trouble you further.'

'The picture of what?' asked Henry Chevron. 'Is it murder yet, or is she still alive?'

The moment after he spoke he knew, again, that it wasn't what he'd have said if he'd thought. Some words are dangerous in themselves. The word murder is so dangerous. But the policeman's regard continued mild.

'Certainly Mrs Parkin is still alive, sir. They've got a very nice cottage hospital. Only she can't just yet give any evidence. Now, sir, if you're willing to help –?'

Henry for a moment thought of demanding his solicitor; but such a course was obviously unnecessary, and irritation had made him behave foolishly enough already. He nodded co-operatively, and the policeman nodded pleasantly back.

'When you called on Mrs Parkin, sir –'

'Wait,' said Henry. 'I didn't call on Mrs Parkin at all. Not in the social sense. I didn't know her, I didn't even know her name, until I saw it in this evening's paper. I went in –'

'You do admit entering, sir?'

'Naturally. I left my name on a paper bag, no doubt you've got it, it's my writing, any expert would prove it. But I don't like the word "admit",' said Henry Chevron. 'I'm not "admitting" anything. I'm . . . relating.'

'It was just a form of speech,' apologized the policeman.

'I still don't like it,' said Henry loudly. He became aware that Catherine was trying to catch his eye, that she wanted to interrupt, and motioned her angrily to silence. He knew he was losing his temper, and that it was foolish, but her interference wouldn't help him to keep it. With an effort, he continued more blandly. 'Let's say, officer, I agree I entered, as you put it, a house called Wychwood Cot, whose owner I didn't know from Adam, yesterday evening on my way back to town, with the idea of buying eggs. Will that do?'

'According to our information, sir, Mrs Parkin didn't sell eggs.'

Henry controlled himself.

'I mistook the directions given me by a young woman farther down the street. Obviously she directed me to Wychwood Farm; I went to Wychwood Cot. The back door being unlatched, I . . . entered. Mrs Parkin – whose identity I did not then know – appeared at the same moment from the orchard.

In the course of an extremely tiresome and fruitless conversation, she being deaf as a door-post, I wrote my name on a paper bag. I then went empty away, leaving the lady, I assure you, uncoshed. I suppose the time –'

'Henry!' cried Catherine.

'Will you, for heaven's sake, leave this to me?' shouted Henry. 'The time, officer, being then probably about six-fifteen.'

The policeman sighed.

'It's a pity, sir.'

'What's a pity?' snapped Henry.

'Mrs Chevron, sir, just told me, just before you came in, you were home last night by six.'

There are moments when the presence of a third party does not in the least inhibit a matrimonial exchange. Henry swung round upon Catherine, his wife, exactly as though they were alone.

'You said I was here? Will you, for heaven's sake, tell me why?'

Catherine straightened her back against the petit-point cushions of the sofa. She'd worked on them for years; the biggest, of her own design, resumed their honeymoon at Majorca – purple bougainvillea trellised against a sunny sky. Latterly she'd turned to classic Tudor birds and beasts.

'I thought perhaps you'd been speeding . . .'

'If I had, what a damn fool way to behave!'

'I'm sorry,' said Catherine.

'You may well be,' retorted Henry furiously. 'You've planted me as number one suspect in a possible murder case.' He swung back to the policeman almost with relief; man to man. 'My wife, officer – and here I'll certainly go on record,

I'd like you to take this down – my wife has behaved like an imbecile. All right, I see you think you're on to something. I'd no motive, I don't need the odd pound from an old woman's handbag, but I see that owing to my wife's idiocy you've grounds for suspicion. Is there any other evidence against me?'

The policeman looked shocked.

'If I may say so, sir, you're going much too fast. We're simply collecting information –'

'Then what else have you collected? Perhaps I can help you again,' said Henry ironically.

'Well, there was a certain amount of shouting and screaming, sir,' said the policeman, delicately. 'Heard by the next-door neighbours, about the time you say you left. Mrs Parkin, to be more precise, screaming "Go away!"'

Henry laughed – he hoped lightly.

'Certainly Mrs Parkin was screaming "Go away!" At me, because she didn't want to sell me eggs. I imagine she screamed pretty freely. If her neighbours had been in the least alarmed, why didn't they come rushing round?'

'They report they were going to, sir. As you say, the lady did scream out a good deal, which is why they weren't quicker, as one might put it, off the mark. But in this case it was more than usual; they were going to come round –'

'But they didn't,' pointed out Henry Chevron.

'No, sir; because it stopped,' said the policeman.

With that he thanked Mr and Mrs Chevron both; observed that he wouldn't ask for a statement just at the moment; added that Mr Chevron probably wouldn't be changing his address, but that if he did Scotland Yard would appreciate notice; and courteously took his leave.

'Now,' said Henry, turning to his wife Catherine, 'tell me why you lied.'

She sat upright against the cushions, but the colour that had come back to her cheeks slowly ebbed again. It should have been a moment of respite: the policeman, so courteously withdrawing, should have left them to tears and anxious consultation perhaps, but to a momentary respite as well. Catherine and Henry each suspected that they had passed simply from one crisis to another; also that the second might prove the more disastrous. But there was nothing for it now but to go on – or so it seemed to Henry Chevron.

'Now tell me why you lied,' repeated Henry Chevron. 'You didn't think I was speeding; I don't, and you know it. So why did you tell that lie?'

Catherine moistened her lips. They weren't pale, because she used a very good lipstick; only the bordering flesh was too white.

'He asked what time you got in . . .'

'I gathered that. Why did you say six? Why did you say I was here at six o'clock?'

'Because I'd told Mrs Whyte you were,' said Catherine.

Henry Chevron stared. The answer simply confounded him. He had to think, he had to think for several moments, before he even identified Mrs Whyte as the woman in the next flat. No particular friend, co-operative, Catherine always said, about taking in groceries, but otherwise negligible . . .

'You told Mrs Whyte,' said Henry blankly, 'that I was here last night at six? When I wasn't? For heaven's sake, why?'

Catherine moistened her lips again.

'Because she heard. I mean she must have. You know how thin these walls are. A man's voice. So when I met her in the corridor just afterwards, and she was just coming out, I knew she'd been there all the time, and I said you were home.'

Henry walked over to the window. The movement had no purpose, it was like a prolonged jerk of the body. His mind, on the other hand, was working smoothly and efficiently; it quite surprised him to find how rapidly he grasped and explored every implication of those few brief sentences. So this was what their years of playing fair had come to, he thought; this was what his wife's playing fair had covered. He could even correct himself; Catherine's infidelity couldn't be of long standing, not years' old, her very foolishness, her flurry before the other woman in the corridor, proved her comparatively fresh to intrigue. Yet in sum, this was what those years had come to . . .

'So when he asked me,' Catherine continued painfully, 'the policeman, I said the same thing again. I hadn't time to think. And even if I had – nothing seemed to have happened last night!' cried Catherine. 'You didn't seem upset about anything! How could I know?'

'Nothing of that matters,' said Henry Chevron.

She was silent.

In the street below the window a bus stopped and several passengers got out. Henry knew most of them by sight; they were the people who always got out of that bus, at that hour, at that place. The man who always carried a bag of fruit carried his bag of fruit. The woman who always wore a red hat wore her red hat. Nothing in the world was changed – outside.

Was it necessary that everything should be changed, within?

'All right,' said Henry Chevron reasonably, 'you had a lover here. You could rely on my being late, it's the classic situation. Do I need to know who the chap is?'

Behind his back Catherine didn't move. He simply felt her looking at him.

'Don't you want to know?'

'I'm not sure,' said Henry – reasonably. 'If it's serious, if you're going to want a divorce, of course I must. Otherwise, perhaps the less I know the better. For instance, if it's anyone I do business with.'

'It would be less brutal if you hit me,' said Catherine.

To his annoyance, she began to cry. Now that he was getting used to the idea, Henry himself found the situation less tragic than it should have been. In fact, it wasn't tragic at all. Their playing fair with each other had become too much like play-acting, their marriage too hollow a thing altogether to shed tears about. Even the academic knowledge that he'd been cuckolded didn't particularly distress Henry Chevron. He didn't feel jealous, only surprised . . .

Henry turned and looked at his wife carefully. It was a long time since he'd regarded her with such attention: he noted in detail the blonde hair, soft skin, delicate profile. At thirty-five, Catherine Chevron's prettiness was still girlish. She was a very pretty woman who looked far younger than her age. Even reddened with weeping, her eyes were pretty eyes. Henry Chevron found himself unmoved. He might have been looking at a stranger – the bestowal of whose prettiness on another man than himself naturally didn't affect him, because he felt no proprietary rights in it.

Evidently their marriage had been over far longer than he'd known.

It would be a relief to give up play-acting. Indeed, now that they could both give up play-acting, Henry didn't see why they shouldn't get along together without any strain at all.

'Did you say you did want a divorce or didn't?' he asked Catherine.

To his surprise, she flinched. (What had she said about being brutal? No husband alive, Henry assured himself, could be behaving with less brutality.) However, she answered sensibly enough.

'No. Not just for an affair. That's all it is. Of course, if you want to divorce me –'

'Not at all,' said Henry, with relief. 'I can't think of a greater nuisance. I've a year's hard work ahead of me, and we're perfectly comfortable.'

'Thank you,' said Catherine. 'Don't you want me to promise anything?'

Henry reflected. The habit of playing fair wasn't yet quite dead, and he himself intended to enjoy the fullest liberty; but he answered chiefly out of indifference.

'Just don't make me look a fool. I shan't come home unexpectedly, and I shan't ask questions.'

'It's Simon Richards,' said Catherine.

The situation was no longer academic.

In one instant, everything was changed again. The fact that he'd been cuckolded, so calmly accepted (in an academic spirit) by Henry Chevron, was no longer a merely academic fact. The anonymous figure of his wife's lover had taken on name and face.

Henry hadn't to think so long as he'd thought before identifying Mrs Whyte. He still had to think a moment. For it must have been at least a year earlier, the night he brought Simon Richards home for cocktails; it was fully six months since his work for Richards Hotels ended – a commission made unexpectedly disagreeable by the manners and personality of their proprietor. Unlike most big men, Simon Richards was a bully, a loud-mouthed believer in keeping his employees on their toes, in fear and trembling. He couldn't bully Henry Chevron, Chevron being as much at the top of his tree as Simon Richards was at the top of his; the whole hotelier-world acknowledged that if anyone could convert four bedrooms into six, and still make them look reasonably spacious, it was Henry Chevron. But Simon Richards bullied everyone else Henry saw him in contact with; working for him had been like working for a slaver . . .

He hadn't been able to bully Henry Chevron; but he'd seduced his wife.

'That oaf!' shouted Henry. He was trembling with rage, choking with disgust; if he'd moved one step towards his wife he would have struck her. 'That sadistic baboon!'

'I know you never liked him,' said Catherine.

Insanely, since it was the worst thing he could do if he wished to keep his control, Henry allowed his thoughts to dwell on Simon Richards' person. Women of naturally coarse taste no doubt found him attractive: he stood six-foot-three in his socks – as no doubt such women frequently saw him – and his great powerful head, blue-jowled, was thatched with curly black hair. Henry Chevron looked suddenly at his wife's hands. Catherine had pretty hands, small and slender. The thought of her running them through those tight black curls nauseated him.

'Your taste is coarser than I realized,' said Henry Chevron. 'Or did he give you diamonds? Have we anything cached away?'

'He never gave me anything,' said Catherine. 'He was lonely and I felt sorry for him.'

'Don't strain my credulity too far,' said Henry. 'Let's settle for incontinence. But not even a garnet?' he mocked. 'Just tears of loneliness, on those pretty little hands?'

'I have tried to keep them nice,' said Catherine. 'I didn't think you noticed.'

The irrelevance of women!

'And you still don't want a divorce?' mocked Henry Chevron.

'I've told you,' said Catherine, 'that it's just an affair. He'd never marry me, because I'm too old. But he's fond of me in his way, and I've grown fond of him. You said you wouldn't ask questions –'

'And I shan't,' agreed Henry Chevron.

At last he moved, violently – but not towards his wife, towards the bedroom.

'I'm leaving you,' said Henry Chevron.

Where now was his placid acceptance of a not uncommon, indeed a classic situation? He plunged into the bedroom, pulled a suitcase from the top of the wardrobe, and began thrusting in shirts. 'See him here as often as you like,' called Henry Chevron, 'but it won't be under my roof! Ring him up now, to say the coast's clear! I'm leaving!' Catherine came running to the door; it gratified him to see that she looked frightened. 'But you can't, you mustn't!' she cried. 'Why not?' demanded Henry – and as she laid a hand to the suitcase struck it roughly away. 'Why not, what's to stop me?'

'Scotland Yard,' said Catherine.

It was almost incredible: for the preceding half-hour Henry had completely forgotten Scotland Yard. He'd completely forgotten his status as number one suspect in a potential murder case.

Catherine sat down on one of the beds. She looked frightened, but she was evidently making a strong effort to keep fear out of her voice – to speak (now that her warning had got through to him) calmly and reasonably. Her voice scarcely shook at all, only her hands.

'That policeman practically warned you, Henry, not to go

away anywhere. I still don't see how they can possibly suspect you, you'd no motive, but if you rush away now, what could look worse?'

Henry sat down opposite her. (He and Catherine had slept in twin beds now for four or five years; the re-furnishing of the bedroom, some four or five years earlier, neatly covering their indifference to each other). He knew that what Catherine said made sense; it also offered him a weapon to wound her with.

'I imagine they wouldn't be suspecting me at all,' said Henry Chevron, 'if that unsophisticated copper hadn't taken you for a faithful wife. Don't faithful wives notoriously alibi their husbands?'

Catherine nodded at once. She didn't cry again; she was thinking. Henry unexpectedly found himself recognizing her attitude – chin on palms, her fingers pushed up into her hair. It had once been a joke between them that he could always tell when she'd been thinking, because it made her hair untidy. Well, now she had something to think about, he told himself bitterly.

'Then perhaps it would be best if you did go,' said Catherine at last. 'But to Scotland Yard first, Henry, to explain why you – why you can't spend another night under the same roof with me. Wouldn't that show them I haven't been alibi-ing you, only myself?'

There was sense in this, too. In a way, as Catherine said, it might be the best thing to do.

'And they can take a statement,' Catherine went on, 'or whatever it is, from Simon. To prove that you weren't here, and he was; and that would explain everything again.'

'You think your lover would co-operate?' asked Henry.

'He'd have to,' said Catherine simply. 'They'd send that policeman, and I'd go with him.'

Examining the implications of this, Henry was astonished to find himself uneasy.

'Wouldn't that pretty well finish everything between you?'

'I suppose it would,' said Catherine. 'I'm still certain, Henry, we've found the right thing to do.'

It was obviously the right thing to do.

Catherine's plan was obviously and eminently sensible. What astonished Henry Chevron now was his own reluctance to adopt it.

He found he didn't want to take the tale of his wife's infidelity to Scotland Yard for no other reason than that she was his wife.

The dragging-in of Simon Richards, distasteful in itself, was doubly distasteful because it would expose Catherine, his wife, as such a pathetic fool. (As she must in her heart know she was to boot. *'He'd never marry me, I'm too old.' 'He's fond of me, in his way ...'*) What a fool she had been! Possibly he, Henry Chevron, was a fool too; but the instinct to protect his wife persisted. For the long and the short of it was, he still thought of Catherine as his wife.

'I'll stay here at any rate for tonight,' said Henry Chevron.

Catherine opened her mouth to speak, hesitated; then –

'You've had no dinner,' she said. 'You must be hungry.'

He was hungry. He hadn't until that moment realized it, but he was famished. It was only half-past seven, but the emotions of the last hour had been punishing.

They ate upstairs in the kitchenette. They could neither of them face the restaurant. (Catherine had been crying too much; Henry was too tired.) There were also twelve fresh eggs ...

Catherine went about the business of making an omelette with great seriousness. She had a little bottle of dried herbs that Henry remembered. It could hardly be the same bottle, but it was the same sort; the sort his tooth-powder came in, that Catherine, in the early years of their marriage, had always seized upon as soon as empty, to scald out and re-fill with herbs or peppercorns. It was a very familiar bottle.

Henry sat down to watch his wife cook for him. He would leave in the morning, but in the meantime, he sat and watched her.

His wife's apron also was familiar – a silly confection of thin green muslin, embroidered over the pocket with a bunch of cherries. Any woman would have known it must have been put away carefully for years, to appear now so fresh; to Henry Chevron it was simply familiar. 'How did it happen?' he wanted to ask – out of purely intellectual curiosity. 'How did it happen that for the last five years we've had nothing to say to each other? I know I've been busy, I've been terribly busy, but how the deuce did it happen?' He naturally didn't utter the words aloud, since he was probably leaving in the morning, but it disconcerted him to see Catherine, as they crossed his mind, suspend the beating of her omelette. It appeared that she could still read his thoughts, just like a wife.

'It's not your fault,' said Catherine. 'I don't even know that it was mine. It just happened, when you got so busy. I've left the butter in the refrigerator, will you take it out?'

They ate in silence. When they'd finished, Henry automatically turned on the radio: a sugary version of the Blue Danube Waltz flowed lusciously forth. Catherine listened a moment, then switched it off. 'I don't want to cry any more,' she said reasonably. 'Shan't I help you wash up?' asked Henry. 'If you won't go to Scotland Yard in the morning, I shall,' said Catherine. 'No, thank you, Henry; I'd rather wash up by myself.'

They hadn't used much crockery, only a plate and knife and fork apiece; like all good cooks, Catherine never washed the omelette pan. She was still in the kitchen nearly two hours later, by herself.

How could the night pass, except uneasily? Henry made up a bed on the sitting-room sofa; Catherine without question brought in blankets for him. Physically he was comfortable enough; only he couldn't sleep. He lay and worried about Catherine, his wife.

For he couldn't see what was to become of her. She herself was evidently under no illusion as to the consequences of what she meant to do. Simon Richards wouldn't forgive the publication of their affair – and to the police! – any more than he, Henry, had forgiven her betrayal of her marriage-vows: out of loyalty to a husband already lost, Catherine was about to lose her lover as well. And she wasn't a woman able to stand alone: her need of masculine support was Victorian – also one of the reasons why Henry Chevron had loved and married her . . .

About midnight, it struck him that Catherine too was probably lying awake, as much in need of comfort as himself.

About one in the morning, he acknowledged that it wasn't because he might be arrested that he, Henry Chevron, needed comfort, but because his marriage to Catherine, for whom he still needed to take thought, had finally come to an end. For all his success in converting four hotel-bedrooms into six – for all his admitted supremacy in the country-club line – he needed someone to take thought for, someone who depended on him. As Catherine couldn't stand alone, no more could he. Their needs were different, but complementary.

At about two, Henry Chevron got up and went quietly to the bedroom door and quietly opened it. He wasn't, he assured himself, seeking comfort in his own distress; he simply wanted to see whether Catherine, awake, required comfort from him. He opened the door as quietly as possible, so that if she slept he wouldn't wake her. But his precautions turned out to be unnecessary; there Catherine stood, just on the other side of the door.

'Can't you sleep either, my darling?'

Which one of them spoke?

Of the case of old Mrs Parkin, coshed and robbed, little more was ever reported. Upon regaining her wits she cleared Henry Chevron almost casually – it was after a man came wanting to buy eggs, related Mrs Parkin, that she'd been annoyed again by a man who wanted to sell her a broom. They were so cheap, however, that she decided to take one; and remembered no more after opening her bag, which had contained four pounds nine shillings and a penny.

It was their policeman who brought the Chevrons this good news, while they still sat at breakfast the following morning – so they ever after thought of him, as 'their' policeman. They pressed coffee upon him, and the last of the fresh eggs; he thanked them but refused with his usual kind authority. He was, in fact, quite unprofessionally happy, to relieve so united a couple from their anxiety. The atmosphere of the Chevron kitchen reminded him of his own cosy breakfasts at home. He didn't in his heart blame Mrs Chevron at all, for lying to him. He was convinced that she had seen the paragraph, but he didn't blame her at all, for the lie she'd told to alibi her husband.

The Girl in the Leopard-skin Pants

As the girl in the leopard-skin pants, wearing her leopard skin pants, entered the dining-room, every masculine eye lifted. So did many a wifely eye, to see how the head-waiter would deal with her. At dinner, at that nice hotel on an island half-an-hour's flight from Athens, the rule was skirts.

It was a very nice hotel indeed. Nice academic couples from Cambridge, Mass., and Oxford, England, reciprocally recommended it. Unmarried daughters often accompanied them; cultured spinsters came in pairs. (The register indeed heavily weighted on the distaff side.) It was such a nice, picturesque, old-fashioned hotel, it hadn't even an elevator – but who cared, gazing from magic casements across a wine-dark sea? For there wasn't a single guest incapable of picking up the Keatsian and Homeric references – unless it was the girl in the leopard-skin pants.

They weren't of course actual pelt, but printed fabric. Stretch. Moulding with extreme neatness and accuracy her small, neat behind . . . On her upper half, over a minute brassière printed to match, she had had at least the grace to add a yellow silk shirt – or was it because at sunset the temperature dropped? In any case, she was still in pants, and though the rule against them wasn't actually written up, (like the rule against drawing more than one bath a day), it was universally respected.

'Mademoiselle – Signorina – Miss,' apologized the head-waiter, 'in the restaurant, at dinner, the management prefers a skirt . . .'

'I haven't got one,' said the girl simply.

It was quite true that she'd arrived off the plane that morning wearing slacks, but so had several of the other women now draped in dirndls left over from Salzburg or do-it-yourself caftans. None however was capable of displaying so neat and engaging a behind.

'Sitting down it wouldn't show,' added the girl. 'Would it?'

'I am sorry, Miss,' said the head-waiter, with unusual feeling in his voice, 'but the management is serious. In the snack-bar, there will always be sandwiches . . .'

The girl in the leopard-skin pants actually sniffed – not as before tears, but at the aroma of a *moussaka* just being served. She sniffed as frankly and wistfully as an urchin outside a baker's, before sadly turning tail.

The silence that followed had a mixed quality; as had the comments that broke it. 'Quite right!' murmured Mrs Pevensey, (Oxford.) 'Then why do I feel a possibly irrational sense of guilt?' mused her husband. 'The poor thing!' exclaimed kind Mrs Powell, (Cambridge.) 'I only hope she gets a double-decker!' 'Minced ham on rye, scrambled egg on top,' defined Professor Powell, rather pushing his *moussaka* about his plate. 'How she ever *got* here –' murmured spinster to spinster. As for Professor René Leclerc (from Montreal), he simply closed his eyes to preserve as long as possible the image of the girl in the leopard-skin pants turning tail. His wife, also French-Canadian, merely laughed.

ACTUALLY how the girl in the leopard-skin pants got there was soon common knowledge, she having confided in the barman. She'd won first prize for a slogan to encourage, as she put it, electricity, and could have taken either under-floor heating or a ten-days' trip to the sun. Her mum preferring a gas-fire anyway, she took the trip. Thus her presence was at least explicable – if not why in that particular hotel; unless an advertising agency and Messrs Cooks betwen them had boobed. It was the fond belief of all habitués that Messrs Cook knew nothing of their little island hide-out at all – but ever since convoying the Kaiser to Jerusalem there wasn't much Messrs Cook didn't know, especially about single-room reservations suddenly cancelled in high season. If there'd been such a reservation cancelled at the Ritz at Madrid, the girl in the leopard-skin pants would probably have been turned out of the Prado.

There was naturally some curiosity, especially among the British restricted to a £50 foreign travel allowance, as to the slogan itself. Mrs Pevensey enquired outright.

'ELECTRICITY, SIMPLICITY, FELICITY!' pronounced the girl in the leopard-skin pants. 'Of course I didn't think of it myself; my boy-friend did.'

She referred to her boy-friend, it was noticed, and discussed, as to some matter-of-course accessory like a hand-bag or wrist-watch: adding, 'He's very clever,' employed much the same tone of voice in which she might have added, 'It's dark brown,' (Or of a wrist-watch, 'It's gold.') No doubt she'd acquired all three before she'd left school, humorously, kindly, agreed all the academic wives – getting in first, before their husbands, with sympathetic good-will; but though she could still tell the time, (not indeed from a wrist-watch, but from a black-faced turnip slung fashionably about her neck), and carry small change in a newly-purchased raffia pouch, what on earth was she to do for her third normal accessory?

'Without a man in the place!' sighed Mrs Pevensey. 'Really one feels quite sorry for the child!'

'You are not very polite to my husband,' observed Madame Leclerc. 'Nor to yours either!'

'I meant, unattached,' apologized Mrs Pevensey.

'One comprehends perfectly what you mean,' said Madame Leclerc. 'They will still no doubt do their best . . .'

Professor Pevensey's best was a suggestion that the girl in the leopard-skin pants might enjoy a little excursion to the Turkish cemetery; but his wife doubted it. Professor Powell actually made the same suggestion – the island's points of interest were limited – and was equally discouraged. 'What she really wants is to go dancing at the Casino – and not with you either, darling!' added Mrs Powell, with the mixture of affection and dampingness he knew all too well. 'Why, you couldn't even reverse!'

'But invite her, *mon cher*, invite her, to the Casino!' urged Madame Leclerc more intelligently. 'I shall not be present, I shall be playing bridge!'

'You were not present either,' returned Professor Leclerc, 'when this morning I offered to erect her beach-umbrella for her. She said, "Thanks ever so, Pop" . . . as one might say "Papa". Or even "Grandpère",' he added wryly. 'I shall feel more dignified playing bridge with you, *chérie!*'

The Pevenseys and Leclercs between them got up a very pleasant bridge four each night. Full of running after their long siestas, they often played until two in the morning – which was about the time the girl in the leopard-skin pants got back from dancing not only at the Casino but at one of the bars with juke-boxes down by the beach.

They needn't have pitied her.

'Goodness, the last hour I've been dancing bare-foot!' she giggled – on her second evening encountering Mrs Pevensey in the foyer and holding up a frayed espadrille in proof.

There was no escort visible. Mrs Pevensey forgot her manners in surprise.

'Who on earth with?'

'My boy-friend,' said the girl in the leopard-skin pants.

3

SHE not only went dancing. As was but natural, her mornings were spent flat out on the beach, but in the late afternoon more than one spinster observed her twirling down hairpin bends – the interior of the island being definitely mountainous, and spinsters often slogging up in search of indigenous flora – on the back of a motor-cycle. Miss Brownrigg and Miss Purcell had actually to leap aside, as the girl in the leopard-skin pants waved to them . . . Of her Lochinvar, all they'd observed was dark goggles and a leather jacket.

'Dear child,' protested Miss Brownrigg (all three by a miracle safe home again), 'whoever takes you pillion at such a breakneck speed?'

'My boy-friend,' said the girl in the leopard-skin pants.

Of course she discarded them on the beach. Her thighs, like her back and shoulders, and her midriff between the minute

145

brassière and the top of a sort of G-string, warmed from café-au-lait to ripe apricot, as she perpetually, religiously oiled herself with the motion of a cat sleeking its fur. Like a cat again, she never entered the water; sometimes she engaged in a little manicure, but chiefly she just oiled herself. — Many a husband, watching her wriggle to get at the space between her shoulder-blades, would have been glad to assist; it was however, and however surprisingly, Caroline Pevensey who came to perform the pleasing office.

Besides a boy-friend, the girl in the leopard-skin pants was used to having a girl-friend. Her girl-friend at home was the same age as herself, nineteen, and worked in the same beauty-parlour. At the hotel, the youngest of the accompanying unmarried daughters was actually Caroline, nearing thirty and in proper academic tradition engaged in re-translating Aesop's Fables for under-eights. However, since there was no one more suitable at hand, one morning on the beach, from under an adjacent umbrella —

'My name's Sylvia,' called the girl in the leopard-skin pants. 'Want to borrow any cuticle-cream?'

'Thanks, I don't use it,' returned Miss Pevensey; and out of politeness added, 'Mine's Caroline.'

'But you ought; it nourishes the roots,' urged Sylvia. 'In a dry climate specially, if you don't nourish the roots your nails haven't a chance. Go on, I get it at cost.'

She got all her cosmetics at cost, from eye-shadow through lipstick down to a toe-nail varnish. Caroline could never be persuaded to borrow any of them, but from sheer force of propinquity, and Sylvia's good-will, became at least a surrogate girl-friend. In the mornings, on the beach, she was as often to be found sharing Sylvia's umbrella as under her own — also of course rubbing oil into Sylvia's back. The latter would gladly have returned the service, except that Caroline, who didn't strip, oiled but her face and throat.

'If you don't tan, I can't see whatever you find to do here,' said Sylvia curiously. 'Don't you ever go dancing either?'

'Oh, often,' said Caroline, 'at home.'

In fact she went two or three times each winter, to the increasingly rare private dances still given for a coming-out or a twenty-first birthday. As she and her contemporaries grew older, even these rare occasions grew rarer. In fact she couldn't be said to go dancing at all, in Sylvia's sense; but she had her pride.

'Well, why not here?'

'I don't know anyone to go with,' said Caroline lightly, 'not that I particularly want to. It isn't sour grapes –'

'That's what people always say,' remarked Sylvia ambiguously. 'I'm sure I don't know why.'

'It's one of Aesop's Fables. – Who do *you* go with?' added Caroline impulsively, with reciprocal and indeed far greater curiousness.

'My boy-friend.'

'You mean he's staying somewhere on the island too?' exclaimed Caroline – fancying herself suddenly enlightened beyond her elders.

But Sylvia shook the blonde bouffant locks religiously set each night on curlers got at cost.

'The prize was only for one. My boy-friend here.'

'You've been quick enough picking him up!' observed Caroline uncontrollably – and the next moment was blushing not only at her own vulgarity, but at the implicit censure. Fortunately Sylvia took no offence.

'Well, I couldn't hang about, could I?' she enquired reasonably, 'with only ten days?' She paused. 'If you ever *should* like to go dancing –'

'Thanks,' said Caroline once again, 'but I honestly don't care for it. I never have. You needn't think I'm the fox without a brush!'

'Goodness, whatever'd a fox want with a brush anyway?' marvelled Sylvia. 'They're not like poodles; aren't they wild?'

'A tail,' glossed Caroline. 'It's another of Aesop's Fables.'

Though their conversation often ran at such cross-purposes, (their fields of reference being so different), they still became friends. It was rather, thought Caroline, like making friends with a puppy; she felt the same slight flattery as at a puppy's spontaneous approach. When the Misses Brownrigg and Purcell again complained of having to leap aside, Caroline retorted that on any Route Nationale in France, or on the Via Aurelia, they wouldn't even have been waved to, before being absolutely mown down . . .

She still had to admit privately that the familiar ambiance of quiet and culture was taking a knock. Even passive on the beach, or occasionally sitting up in the attitude of the Little Mermaid at Copenhagen, the girl in the leopard-skin pants disturbed the peace, causing umbrella-shaded husbands to rise and wander instead of reposefully storing energy against the next academic term. Their wives broke off reading *Hyperion* or *The Magic Mountain* to worry about them. The spinsters, however unjustly, pretended peaceful botanizing no longer on. Above all, the whole nice, quiet, culturally-oriented hotel prickled with plain vulgar curiosity . . .

There was of course one obvious way of finding out whom the girl in the leopard-skin pants went dancing with, and that was to go to the Casino and look. What inhibited was the general consensus in favour of ignoring the Casino altogether

148

as un-Keatsian, un-Homeric, and commercial. Only on the eve of Sylvia's departure, and the Pevensey-Leclerc bridge-game having fallen rather into the doldrums –

'Why not stroll down to the Casino?' suggested Madame Leclerc.

Under such a brilliant full moon, why not indeed? Professor and Mrs Powell were equally, easily, persuaded from their backgammon; and all strolled down to the Casino together.

4

THERE rather taking the centre of the floor was the girl in the leopard-skin pants indeed – the Casino apparently having no objection to pants. Her boy-friend was harder to pin-point; she danced with half-a-dozen partners – all by contrast rather natty in sharply-cut suits and brilliantly white shirts, each profiled like an Achilles, but evidently without an Achilles' heel . . .

'Obviously indigenous,' noted Professor Pevensey.

'Where she *finds* them –!' marvelled his wife.

'But they are really *chic*!' exclaimed Madame Leclerc. 'Why have not *I* ever encountered such types?'

'Perhaps because we stay in too nice an hotel to attract gigolos,' said Professor Leclerc. 'Another year, *chérie*, I will take you to the Riviera!'

Suddenly the girl in the leopard-skin pants was leading a sort of Samba – ('Or chorean dance?' glossed Professor Powell) – that promised to turn into a bacchanal. By this time she in turn had spotted her fellow guests from the hotel, and waved to them each time she swung past. In fact she more than waved, she beckoned . . .

'*I* think it's time we all went back,' said Mrs Powell.

'Since we are obviously too old to participate without loss of dignity,' said Madame Leclerc, 'I agree with you!'

Of course Mrs Pevensey and Mrs Powell and Madame couldn't be allowed to walk back alone; and though any one professor might have done triple-duty, so to speak, and left his colleagues behind, none made the offer. It was still such a beautiful night – the air so warm and balmy, moon high, a tideless sea gently lapping – the brief promenade was enjoyed by all; at a flower-stall still open Professors Pevensey and Powell bought their wives bunches of violets, and Professor Leclerc for Madame a gardenia. Under the moon, the wrinkled flower-woman looked like a Sybil; it was a disappointment to all three classicists that she appeared not to understand a word of their thanks couched in Ancient Greek. Most of the guests at the hotel were stronger in Classics than Demotic – in the tongue of Sophocles rather than that of stall-holders – which made any real contact with the islanders, however desirable, uncommonly difficult . . .

'We arrive here,' said Professor Leclerc suddenly, 'and steep ourselves, we imagine, in Grecian influences; but what do we know of Greeks? For years now I have arrived here; is there a single habitant of whose thoughts and feelings I know anything whatever?'

'There must always be a barrier,' said his wife comfortably, 'needing probably a Demotic-speaking psychiatrist to over-leap! Good night, messieurs, mesdames!'

5

FOR little more than a week had the disturbance lasted; on the day of Sylvia's departure, as on that of her arrival, emotions were mixed: not a male but was sorry to see her go, not a female, (unless Caroline), but felt happier. The Pevenseys and Powells and Leclercs however all lingered in the foyer before going down to the beach to wish her *bon voyage*.

By chance, no one else was taking the plane. Standing alone beside her slight baggage, she had a waifish look.

'My dear, I do hope you've enjoyed yourself?' said kind Mrs Powell.

'One could see she did!' chuckled Madame Leclerc.

The girl in the leopard-skin pants, (now actually wearing slacks again), looked simply surprised.

'We were afraid you might find it dull,' explained Mrs Pevensey, 'without a man in the place . . .'

'But it's been *fabulous*!' protested the girl. 'There were eleven!'

'*Eleven?*' repeated Mrs Powell.

'Including kitchen-staff. Actually Theo who does the grills dances best of all – *and* has the best motor-cycle. It's a Honda. Then there's Cyril and Nick and Alex, and George and Hector, and Lysander and Spiros – he's on your table – and Basil and Chris and Phil.'

Light dawned at last.

'You mean you've been going dancing with the *waiters?*' exclaimed Mrs Pevensey.

'Why, didn't you recognize them?' asked Sylvia, surprised. again. 'Of course they look different in their good suits, and Theo you wouldn't have seen – but Spiros I made sure you did! It's his mother who keeps the flower-stall,' she added. 'It's why it's open so late; she needs every penny because his brother's in hospital. Cyril and Chris help out a bit, because they're cousins.'

'And Hector and Lysander?' suggested Professor Lecterc.

'*They* want to emigrate and open a Greek restaurant. Either in London or New York. Of course I didn't encourage them; life off the island's much tougher than they think. I know. Beauty-parlours are just jungles. This holiday's been my first lucky break ever – except I s'pose that I've always had a boy-friend!' said the girl in the leopard-skin pants.

At that moment her taxi arrived. She gave Caroline a sudden hug and nipped in. As the vehicle passed the terrace below she leant out to wave; Theo and Spiros, Philip and Alex, in fact the whole restaurant and kitchen staff bar the head-waiter, number-ing altogether eleven, were lined up to wave back.

5

'MIGHTN'T I have guessed it?' mused Mrs Powell. 'Don't half our college boys at home wait on table in the vacation?'

'Only these aren't college boys,' said her husband, 'and I positively refuse to identify my students with your Greeks on the make.'

'They made nothing out of that girl,' observed Madame Leclerc. 'Except good advice! – to remain here on their island collecting tips! (Do not forget when we leave, *mon cher*, the brother in hospital!) But tell us your opinion,' she asked Caroline, 'you who knew her better than any of us? Did she imagine it was with college boys she went dancing?'

'No,' said Caroline.

'Not a Demotic-speaking psychologist either?' proposed Professor Leclerc, with an eye on his wife.

'No,' repeated Caroline slowly. 'I think she just thought of waiters as being people too. I'm sorry now I didn't let her take *me* dancing.'

Behind her back the head-waiter, rarely on duty so early, slightly coughed. For so mature and important-looking a man it was surprising that he wore no wedding-ring; equally surprising, the lightness with which he carried his imposing bulk. Broad-shouldered and heavy-hipped, he none the less looked capable of dancing. He also spoke perfect English.

'I don't get shot of the bunch in the restaurant much before midnight,' he murmured, 'but if I might subsequently have the pleasure of escorting you –'

Caroline turned just sufficiently to nod.

Though the Pevenseys themselves stayed but a week longer, there is now an extremely successful Greek restaurant in Oxford.

The Amethyst Cat

EVERYONE KNOWS THAT in 1860 far too much looting went on at the Summer Palace in Pekin. Bric-à-brac carved from jade and crystal proved in particular irresistibly attractive to an acquisitive if not licentious soldiery. (Today, of course, such objects would probably be described as having been liberated.) The result was the dispersal through Western Europe of a great number of miniature Chinese masterpieces; and Sherrard, some hundred years later, thought he had his eye on one of them.

Sherrard looked through the plate glass window at the cat, and the cat, or so it seemed, looked back through the window at Sherrard.

It was a portly and sagacious creature; couchant in an attitude of great comfort and dignity; about nine inches long by five high, carved from a block of amethyst quartz which must thus have been considerably larger. The body was light grey, striated with crystal, the mask and ears violet – almost Siamese colouring; but the broad complacent face, sunk so reposefully upon the broad chest, had nothing of a Siamese's nervous tension. It was a Chinese cat – and, in Sherrard's opinion, a masterpiece.

Sherrard at this junction, it so happened, greatly desired to make a gift of surpassing beauty to a young Chinese lady, resident in New York. He therefore entered the shop, and a moment or two later balanced the creature on his palm.

He could just manage it. For its size, it was astonishingly

heavy. It must have weighed about seven pounds. It was also astonishingly cold – like wet ice.

'Amethyst quartz?' suggested Sherrard.

'Amethyst quartz,' agreed the proprietress, with a polite smile for her customer's knowledgeableness. She was a small, elegant woman, thus matching her establishment, which was situated in Piccadilly; for his pocket's sake Sherrard would have preferred less *chic*, but at the same time recognized that one couldn't expect such a cat to turn up in – to put up with – any flea-market. 'Of the finest quality,' added the proprietress. 'So is the workmanship. Turn him over.'

Sherrard obeyed. The cat's underside was as exquisitely carved as the rest of him: four delicate paws, the claws withdrawn, were tucked neatly into a comfortable belly. Near the root of the tail Sherrard made out a small, faintly-incised Chinese ideogram.

'Have you its pedigree?' enquired Sherrard, without irony.

The proprietress shrugged.

'Chinese and, say, eighteenth century. Not that I'm an expert. I bought it at a sale in a country house, because I was lucky, there were no Chinese experts there. And, of course, I know what my eyes tell me, it's the work of a considerable artist.'

Sherrard's eyes told him the same thing. He appreciated it, it gave him confidence, that she didn't produce any tale of loot from the Summer Palace to put the price up. In any case, the price was quite high enough for Sherrard.

'Two hundred pounds,' mumured the proprietress indifferently.

'I'll have to think,' said Sherrard. 'May I let you know tomorrow?'

. . . . .

Indeed he had to think. He was a foreign correspondent, and a successful, even a celebrated one; on his pay and expenses he lived a thoroughly ample life; but to put down two hundred pounds cash – six hundred dollars, two hundred thousand francs, three hundred and fifty thousand lire – wasn't a trifle to him. All the rest of that day, and well into the night, he mulled it over.

There were several reasons why he wished to make Maria in New York some exquisitely beautiful gift. In the first place she was herself exquisitely beautiful, and like to like. (Her Chinese name meant Small Pink Lotus Bud at Dawn, and it suited her. Maria discarded it to become Maria when she so thankfully and enthusiastically became an American citizen.) Had he been a millionaire, and had he known nothing of Maria but her appearance, Sherrard would have bought her the amethyst cat as a mere matter of artistic propriety. But he did, besides, know her, he'd known her off and on for some years, and had the greatest admiration for her character also. Educated in China, at a Quaker school, sent on a scholarship to an American university, it perhaps hadn't been difficult for Maria herself to acquire citizenship in the New World; but with incredible pains and persistence, as soon as she could support a dependant, she succeeded in bringing over her only living relative – an uncle so old and so useless that only a heart of gold could see him as anything but a burden. 'He was kind to me when I was little,' said Maria, 'and I've got him off opium on to Coca-Cola!'

For as well as being golden-hearted and beautiful, she was sensible and strong-minded. She had every feminine quality. Every time he left New York without asking her to marry him, Sherrard regretted it in the 'plane.

Why he didn't ask her to marry him was partly because he

was so used to being a bachelor, and partly because Maria kept him always, very slightly, at a distance. She kept everyone, Sherrard fancied, slightly at a distance. In the children's hospital where she worked as a masseuse she had dozens of friends, but no intimates; as she had dozens of escorts, but no one particular escort. Her reserve was like a delicate Chinese fan fluttering perpetually before her face, which she couldn't cast aside even though she wanted to. Sherrard thought that at the sight of the amethyst cat – so surpassingly beautiful, expensive and Chinese – perhaps that fan would for an instant drop; never, if he seized his chance, to be picked up again . . .

He went back to the shop next day, and wrote out a cheque.

Sherrard had known all along that he was buying no common cat; the personality it developed, on the flight out to New York, was none the less disconcerting. It created difficulties, and attracted attention, all the way.

To begin with, he hadn't cared to pack it in his luggage. It was too precious, and possibly too fragile. (It might have survived at least a century of racketing about, and perhaps a century before that; Sherrard still thought of it as fragile, because precious.) So he stuffed it into his over-night bag, where its weight, on the airport scales, produced a startled query from the officer in charge. 'It's a cat,' said Sherrard shortly. 'I've a cat in my bag.' Someone to the rear laughed, but the officer looked grim. 'Livestock?' he enquired sternly. 'No, quartz,' snapped Sherrard. He pulled it out; the officer grinned and passed him – on payment of excess; and as they were immediately marshalled to their 'plane, Sherrard boarded it with the cat under his arm.

Unusually, the seat beside him remained vacant. Having dumped the cat down on it, he left it there. The cat settled down very comfortably but continued to attract attention. Sherrard was reminded of the one and only flight he'd made with his Aunt Gertrude – a charming and sociable old lady who'd apparently regarded the whole trip as a nice At Home given by the air line. Like his Aunt Gertrude (which was something), the cat made contact only with the nicest people; chiefly elderly ladies travelling with their husbands. One such couple – whom Sherrard mentally christened The Texans, on no other grounds than the man's broad-brimmed hat and general air of prosperity – sat directly across the aisle; the lady in particular was perfectly charmed by the cat and the cat, it couldn't be denied, appeared most complacently to receive her attentions. It didn't purr, it couldn't, but it appeared to purr. Finally Sherrard, who unlike Aunt Gertrude felt no social obligations whatever, covered it over with his scarf.

He was none the less roused from sleep, shortly before arrival, by the Texan.

'Pardon me, I thought you were awake,' the Texan apologized.

'At least I should be,' said Sherrard – his Aunt Gertrude, as it were reminding him of his manners.

'The fact is, my wife's taken a remarkable fancy to your cat. If I could get one similar for her, I'd be very glad to know where to go for it.'

'I'm sorry, I'm afraid this one's about two hundred years' old,' said Sherrard.

The Texan looked at it respectfully. (Somehow, during the night, it had got its head out again.)

'You mean no one makes them nowadays?'

'Not that I know of,' said Sherrard.

'Too bad,' said the Texan regretfully. 'All the same, I'd like you to take my card – just to show Maisie I'm trying. If you ever run across another, and have the kindness to let me know, I'll be deeply obliged.'

Sherrard pocketed the bit of pasteboard and tried to doze off again. But he'd been disturbed, for a man of his fifty years, too thoroughly; instead he sat and thought about Maria.

The cat dozed off all right. Sherrard didn't remember pulling the scarf over its head a second time, but when he looked again, not an ear showed. It was thus in fine fettle to make an exhibition of itself at the customs; but, leaning on its age, carried Sherrard through without difficulty.

Sherrard reached Maria's flat about seven that evening. There were several professional contacts he had needed to make first; he'd had no time to get the cat wrapped, as he'd thought of doing, in some elegant packing. It was still simply muffled in his scarf. But as he set it down so muffled, on the little table in the centre of her living-room, it presented at least an intriguing shape.

Maria was there waiting for him. He'd cabled her. Actually he'd cabled her twice – once from London, once from Gander.

'You are the nicest friend in the world!' cried Maria. There was still, even in the pretty, affectionate phrase, a formality: as though she offered a little poem of welcome brushed across a fan. She stood before him none the less so exquisitely beautiful, so explicitly friendly, that his heart rose. 'And you've brought me a present from England!' cried Maria. 'Really, you're too good!'

Smiling and eager, she poked at the bundle with a tentative forefinger. It was another of her charming traits that she was readily pleased, and always showed her pleasure; yet Sherrard had no doubt that she reserved pleasure still in store, so to speak, that she would find the unimaginably right words of gratitude and admiration, when she saw his marvellous gift, that before the cat, her compatriot, in short, the fan of reserve would at last drop.

Already she was more eager, more caught up by a flow of pleasure and excitement, than he had ever seen her.

'Do I unwrap it, or do you show it me?' demanded Maria. 'I'm not going to guess, I'm too impatient!'

'Sit down, and I'll put it in your lap,' said Sherrard.

Obediently, Maria sat. She even (to give *him* pleasure) closed her eyes – and this momentarily distracted Sherrard, for he had never before seen Maria with her eyes shut. She looked at once ageless, and very young; her lids were the colour of tea-roses; and with irrational tenderness Sherrard realized that her lashes weren't long, as he'd always believed them to be, but quite short and scrubby, like little brushes . . .

'What are you waiting for?' urged Maria.

Sherrard pulled the cat out of its wrapping and set it down on her knee, between her slim welcoming hands.

For an instant, undoubtedly, as she opened her eyes, the fan dropped. But only for an instant. Almost immediately her features recomposed themselves into an expression of extreme politeness.

'How perfectly *lovely*,' said Maria.

Sherrard picked up the table-lamp and held it so that the light shone down through the violet ears.

'It's amethyst quartz.'

'I see it is. Lovely!' repeated Maria. With quick, intelligent fingers, she traced the curve from nape to tail, tipped the cat over, scrutinized its underneath, and settled it back between her palms.

'Oh, dear, I hope you didn't pay too much for it!' cried Maria uncontrollably . . .

Then Sherrard knew that the emotion she'd so briefly betrayed had indeed been what he'd fancied it. For a moment, incredulously, he'd fancied she was disappointed. Now he knew she was.

'Does that mean it's no good?'

'Of course not! It's beautiful! Only if they told you it was eighteenth century, you might have paid four or five hundred dollars.'

Sherrard was very quick-witted. He saw what was coming and got in first.

'Of course it's only a modern reproduction.'

Maria smiled with relief.

'I'm so glad you weren't robbed – as people can be, quite shockingly! Now I can enjoy my present with a good conscience!'

She jumped up, and set the cat first on the table again, then on a tabouret, then on the mantelpiece, seeking where it would look best; she gaily and charmingly made a fuss of it, even giving it a vase of violets to smell at, a little silver box to play with. Nothing could have been prettier; but Sherrard remained unhappy. He was indeed in a most distressing quandary; the sheer costliness of the gift had been a large part of its point – a declaration, so to speak, of his intentions; yet he couldn't now admit to it without also admitting himself a sucker – worse, without bringing down on his head Maria's mingled sympathy and exasperation. She had always an acute dislike of any kind of waste – in her early days in America Sherrard recalled how she'd worried over the crusts cut off from sandwiches – and waste of money ranked next with her to waste of food. She was very nearly parsimonious. Considering her starveling infancy, the trait was a natural one; for the first time Sherrard found himself disliking it. He hadn't toted the cat half-way round the world to have its price asked! True, Maria hadn't done so yet, in so many words, but Sherrard strongly suspected her of wanting to, certain of finding it exorbitant in any case . . .

He also suspected – too late, too late! – that she didn't much care for the cat at all.

'Next time I'll bring you a cashmere twin-set,' said he.

Undeniably, her eyes sparkled.

'Will you really? I'll give you my size.'

It didn't soothe Sherrard's soreness that the cat meanwhile continued to sit handsome and complacent as ever, looking every minute of two hundred years' old. It met Sherrard's gaze affably. 'All right, so you fooled me,' thought Sherrard. (It didn't, oddly enough, occur to him that he might have been fooled by the shop-keeper; he was convinced that the cat had fooled them both.) 'But now you've run into an expert,' thought Sherrard nastily, 'and as soon as I'm out of town you'll be put in your proper place . . . which is probably the back of a clothes-closet.'

Naturally the cat's expression didn't alter. Maria exclaimed afresh, that very moment, at its air of aplomb. Sherrard gave the impostor another dirty look, for his own aplomb left much to be desired – he having not realized the implications of his hasty threat. '*As soon as I'm out of town*,' he'd warned the cat; did he then mean to leave cat and Maria together behind him? Wasn't he after all going to ask Maria to be his wife? And if not, why not? Because she'd wanted to know how much he'd paid for her present? Put so, the thing was ridiculous; there stood Maria just as exquisite as he remembered her, just as charmingly affectionate, having moreover, and at last, dropped the fan of her reserve – to reveal behind it the admirable wifely quality of concern for a man's pocket . . .

What an admirable wife she would make!

She'd probably run a wonderfully economical kitchen.

Not impossibly, when he wanted to go out on the town, she'd have something in the oven.

She'd certainly want to see any dinner-bill.

Sherrard glanced again at the amethyst cat, and the cat with ancient wisdom gazed back at Sherrard. (With *fictitiously* ancient wisdom, Sherrard reminded himself.) It was shocking, and it was completely out of period, that the cat appeared to murmur something under its whiskers about wives to keep men steady, but concubines to keep them young. For a moment Sherrard felt he should absolutely apologize to Maria for the cat's immorality; but on second thoughts recognized that to her a lump of quartz, however masterly carved, remained simply a lump of quartz.

Which brought him to another point. Beautiful Maria – sensible and kind Maria – lacked imagination. 'And what else do I deal in?' Sherrard asked himself. 'I, the factual reporter, what else after all do I deal in? Don't I produce, for those who haven't the wit or opportunity to make them for themselves, the images of President, Prime Minister, statesman? Don't I image the whole world, or try to, in a column of print? Maybe it would be all right for me, maybe it would be even good for me, to marry a wife with no imagination at all; but somehow I don't think so . . .'

Complacently upon Maria's mantelpiece sat the amethyst cat.

Sherrard turned back to Maria. He didn't know how long the silence had lasted, only that it had lasted quite long enough. 'Where would you like to go for dinner?' he asked uneasily.

Now Maria, damn it, was looking uneasily at *him*.

'My dear, I hate to tell you,' she apologized, 'but actually I've a date already. And it's one I can't put off – with a boy from China, a boy who knew my family there . . . It's his first evening in New York, you see, without me he won't know what to do with himself. You do understand, don't you?'

'Perfectly,' said Sherrard. 'You'll see he isn't robbed.'

Maria laughed in happy relief.

'That among other things! Though tonight I think he wants to be rather grand and extravagant, to celebrate *getting* here!'

'Just for once I don't suppose it matters,' suggested Sherrard, 'if you keep him on a tight rein afterwards?'

'Oh, I mean to,' agreed Maria seriously. (No wonder the cat looked smug. 'That's the sort of lad for *her*,' it seemed to say, 'a lad she can boss about; see what I've saved you from!' Sherrard ignored the brute.) 'So I really ought to dress up a little,' added Maria, now glancing frankly at the clock, 'but won't you wait and meet him? He is studying medicine, and he seems to be really quite brilliant . . . Please wait!'

'If you want me to, of course I will,' said Sherrard amiably.

He felt suddenly flat – flat and sore. He wasn't yet grateful to the cat at all. He felt let down. For nothing had turned out as he'd planned; even his own emotions had gone adrift, he didn't even feel jealous of the boy from China; and it wasn't exactly Maria's fault, so that he couldn't even feel angry with Maria. His anger turned itself upon the cat – upon the smug imposter he'd toted half round the world, with no other result than to put himself, Sherrard, in danger of looking a fool . . .

'What's the Chinese name that means Labour-in-Vain?' Sherrard mentally enquired of the amethyst cat. 'You should know; it's yours.'

·   ·   ·   ·   ·

He had been alone perhaps five minutes (while Maria dressed up) when the door discreetly opened. The old party who now joined him, however, was in appearance at least less discreet than showy. Maria's efforts to turn her uncle into a hundred per cent American had in one respect succeeded only too well: he wore a Palm Beach shirt. There were hibiscus blossoms upon it, also sea-horses, also bathing-beauties, but above its brilliant uninhibited colouring a face like an old walnut peered, incongruously diffident, humble and submissive.

'I beg pardon,' murmured Maria's uncle. 'I did not know anyone was present . . .'

'Don't go, come on in and keep me company,' said Sherrard. 'I'm just waiting to vet Maria's new beau.'

It was as incongruous to him, that slangy turn of phrase, as was the Palm Beach shirt on Maria's uncle. Sherrard recognized it at once, recognizing also that he wasn't quite himself. Fortunately the old man, it seemed, recognized nothing but a permission to enter; he sidled in bowing politely, with a smile that revealed a really splendid set of false teeth. Sherrard was again aware of an incongruity: they were so wonderfully confident, those splendid American dentures, yet the old man's smile remained humble . . .

'Your company will give me great pleasure,' Sherrard corrected himself. 'Perhaps you remember me? My name is Sherrard.'

Extraordinarily, to this overture there was no response at all.

The old man mightn't even have heard. It was extraordinary indeed – one moment all his attention was fixed on Sherrard, the next it had flown away; one moment his eyes dropped humbly before the stranger, the next they were riveted on the mantelpiece. With short, hasty steps he almost trotted across the room; pushed his wrinkled old face against the smooth complacent countenance of the cat, laid his fingers (like a bundle of bamboo twigs) to the curve of the cat's nape, tipped the beast over, scrutinized its belly – and only then turned back to Sherrard.

Maria had always insisted on her uncle speaking correct English, so that he could never say anything very quickly; but the words got out at last. 'How – came – this – object – here?'

'I brought it to give Maria,' said Sherrard. 'D'you like it?'

'I *made* it!' proclaimed Maria's uncle triumphantly. 'See, under, my mark!'

There was now naturally much Sherrard understood that he hadn't before. His thoughts raced. Poor Maria, to begin with! – had she recognized her uncle's mark too, or only his general style? Or even remembered, perhaps, sitting under his work-bench as he chipped and polished and engraved at that very beast? In whichever case, what a facer for her, what a grotesquely absurd disappointment! And how well, in the circumstances, she'd behaved! Sherrard felt all his affection for her flooding back – not too strongly, not strongly enough to make him jealous of her Chinese beau – but with sufficient warmth to heal all soreness. 'Poor Maria, it's a wonder she didn't box my ears!' thought Sherrard – and began to laugh.

Maria's uncle had been laughing for some time. He stood and rocked with silent, delighted laughter, the cat clasped to his bosom, all humility wiped from his face by an artist's giddy pride. Even his teeth looked very nearly natural.

'Listen,' said Sherrard, 'I'm taking that cat away from Maria and giving it to you. *Back* to you. You understand? It's yours. If you want to sell, I can give you an address where they'll probably pay anything you like to ask for it. And if you can lay hands on any more quartz, or whatever else you carve

166

cats out of, I imagine you've a very rewarding future. I see I'll
have to say all this over again,' concluded Sherrard, 'so in the
meantime, instead of waiting for Maria's wonderboy, why
shouldn't we go out to dinner ourselves?'

There was a response, all right, then. Half incredulous, half
eager, like a very old tortoise sniffing the spring, Maria's uncle
poked forth his head above the cat's. 'You and I go out to
dinner?'

'Why not?' said Sherrard.

'Chinese style?'

'Why not? We needn't,' added Sherrard, as the old man
appeared to turn something over in his mind, 'disturb Maria.
We'll just leave her a note.'

But it wasn't Maria the old man was thinking of. Stroking a
finger down the cat, nose to tail. 'You are certain,' he pressed,
'it can be sold for much? For how much? A – hundred
dollars?'

'Six hundred,' said Sherrard – justifiably confident in his
Texan.

Every tooth in the old head gleamed anew.

'Then *you* shall be *my* guest, not I yours,' pronounced
Maria's uncle.

What an evening it was!

All the best dinners, Sherrard remembered once hearing, are
eaten on credit; the old man's credit with a certain compatriot
restaurateur appeared illimitable – especially after he had
displayed the amethyst cat, which they bore with them. (It
didn't even have to suffer the indignity of being left in pawn.)
They dined, with intervals for conversation while special
dishes were being cooked, or special delicacies sent for, until
well past midnight. Sherrard was rather queasy next day and

so, as reported by Maria, was her uncle. 'Where did you two go for heaven's sake?' demanded Maria, over the telephone. 'And why didn't you stay to meet Harry? We were disappointed.'

'Didn't you and Harry have a good time too?' asked Sherrard.

'Yes, of course we did,' said Maria. 'We had a wonderful time; we ate steak. But my uncle tells me you've given him my cat, he says now it's his!'

'As you always knew it was,' said Sherrard.

There was a slight pause. Then to his immense satisfaction – what a splendid girl she was! – he heard Maria giggle. 'How could I tell you? But really it's the nicest thing that ever happened, my uncle is so pleased! And what do you think he means to do *now*?'

'I know; we spent last night planning it,' said Sherrard. 'He is going to go back to carving cats, and make hundreds of dollars, and put them all away in a box, and write on it, "*For Maria's Dowry*" . . .'

Sherrard himself boarded the east-bound 'plane as usually unwed – or affianced – but not unhappy either. He hadn't even the amethyst cat with him; but both felt better off as they were, and at least it made for a peaceful journey. He was indeed two hundred pounds to the bad, which he could ill afford; but there had been something to show for it. An old man's face of bliss, as he looked down at his no longer useless hands: an old man's joy in dowering the kind child who'd succoured him . . .

'Cheap at the price,' thought Sherrard; glared disagreeably at his neighbours, in case any should be minded to address him, and went to sleep.

At the Fort Flag

THE FORT FLAG Hotel was not the sort of place in which Professor and Mrs Brocard were usually to be found. It was outrageously expensive, and Brocard's salary did not permit extravagance; it was also rather brazen in its display of luxury and attracted a clientèle rather brazen in the display of wealth. The big garage was full of new cars, the evening dresses on the terrace before dinner came from Paris; while the two cocktail-bars were so perpetually crowded that many guests (Mrs Brocard calculated) must have doubled their bills for accommodation by their bills for drinks. In short, the whole place, in post-war England, was a financial phenomenon only to be explained by the fact that very few guests, besides the Brocards themselves and their friend Charles Harbin, ever paid a second visit. Each summer the beautiful ladies and their sleek escorts, the stout matrons, often with children, but husbandless save at the week-end – each summer all these characters looked the same, but were in fact different: it was as if a fixed sum of loose spending-money annually changed hands. 'No doubt they all prey upon one another,' observed Professor Brocard placidly. 'A primitive sort of existence . . .'

The Brocards, however, had to be careful. Their budget allowed only beer for the Professor, while his wife, because he left her alone all day, was awarded a sherry before dinner. The reason Janet Brocard was left alone was also the reason why they stayed at the hotel: it adjoined one of the best golf-courses in the country, and Brocard, who in his youth had been runner-up for the Amateur Championship, still boasted in his fifties a handicap of one. Charles Harbin had a handicap of three. Each morning the two men set out to play eighteen holes before lunch, (a frugal snack of sandwiches, to save expense), and eighteen after; and this annual three weeks' orgy was the great indulgence of the Professor's life. But his wife did not play, and though he was frankly glad of it, Brocard felt it only fair that she should be indulged also: hence the splendours of the Fort Flag, which provided her, as Janet herself was first to agree, with a thorough change.

And indeed she found the peaceful, idle, uninterrupted days very agreeable. Her normal life was almost too full: she ran a house single-handed, coached half-a-dozen history students, and took a fair share in all university activities. At the Fort Flag, with nothing to do but look on, Janet Brocard's alert and uncantankerous mind found perpetual amusement, while her body took a good rest. She swam, just a little, and walked, just a little, and worked a little at her *gros point* – or at any rate held it on her knee, for this gay piece of needlework, into which scarcely a stitch was put save at the hotel, there became one of her greatest assets. It provided her, so to speak, with a character: she was the lady who did embroidery. Janet did not at all want to be known as the lady who wrote about Merovingians, and though the positive fact might never have come out, she could not help looking suspiciously clever: the bright wools in her lap, the thimble on her finger, saved her from the stigma of being a high-brow and attracted nothing but good will. 'What patience!' approved her fellow guests. 'How beautifully you do it!' – and passed benevolently on into the bars. The young were particularly enthusiastic: they liked to see a middle-aged lady so suitably and contentedly employed. 'I wish *my* mother did that,' observed one semi-naked nymph, pausing to lean a smooth brown thigh against Janet's chair. The parent in question, hardly more fully clad, was even then hooting impatiently in the family sports car. 'It's a hobby for old age,' explained Janet kindly. 'I've only just taken to it myself . . .'

Each evening, after the Professor and Charles Harbin had described to Janet all that had happened on the golf-course, Janet in turn described all that had happened in the hotel. The two men – Brocard was a geologist, and Harbin an authority on vegetable pests – listened with interest and surprise, and also with admiration; for even on the first night of a stay Janet could supply more information than either male, industriously, would have gathered in a month.

2

'THIS year,' reported Janet, accepting her pre-dinner sherry on the terrace, 'we've a Beauty Queen. She's the most beautiful typist in south-west England, picked by the *Daily Flash* from more than a thousand competitors. She's the one in the white play-suit.'

'Healthy little creature,' said Brocard. 'Did they find out if she could type?'

'Certainly she can type. She can type ninety words a minute. A fortnight here was part of the prize, and that's the Beauty Editress, with blue hair, chaperoning her. But it's rather unlucky, because we've also a film starlet, who is stealing her thunder. She's the one in yellow.'

'I think I prefer the starfish,' said Harbin.

'I don't see how you can distinguish,' objected Brocard.

'She looks tidier.'

'You mean more *soignée*,' corrected Janet. 'The man with her leads a dance-band, and those are our celebrities. The rest are just usual run-of-the-mill – but I must say I think they're colourful.'

The Professor, who always took his wife's opinions seriously, refocused his attention from the particular to the general and slowly turned his gaze from one end of the terrace to the other. Janet, as usual, was right: under the coloured umbrellas, under the coloured awnings of the bar, more varied colours of clothing, hair and skin, of fabrics and cosmetics, shifted like a kaleidoscope. A few of the guests had already changed for dinner; the rest wore shorts, beach-wear or sarongs; and save for a couple of dinner-jackets the darkest tone discernible was the brilliant orange-tan of a man's sailcloth trousers. Not all costumes were appropriate: a stout matron had no business in a lilac play-suit: but the lilac, as colour, lay as exquisitely against her fat brown flesh as did the scarlet ribbons against a girl's blonde hair. Colour was its own justification; and with a grunt of approval the Professor turned back to his wife.

'Yes,' he said, 'it's a bright paint-box . . . Have you brought your stripes?'

Janet laughed. Her striped dinner-dress appeared as regularly at the Fort Flag as did her embroidery.

'I'm going to change into it now,' she said, 'to dazzle you both at dinner.'

But before they all went in they paused to watch, over the back of the terrace, the arrival of the hotel station-wagon. Only one guest, it appeared, had come by the late train: a solitary young woman in a dark travelling-coat. She had a good deal of luggage, and while it was unloading the Brocards saw her stand a moment and look about, as though taking her bearings. The drive lay some feet below the level of the terrace, which was properly approached only through the hotel; but a short brick stair built against the retaining wall provided a back way up. This, after a brief hesitation, the new-comer quietly mounted; and again stood to look round. In all this there was nothing particularly strange: what was strange was the peculiar, the discriminating quality of the girl's glance.

The head of the stair opened no more than a yard or so from where the Brocards and Charles Harbin had paused; they were the first three persons to come under the girl's eye; yet she did not appear to see them. Or rather she saw, and at the same instant dismissed them; her gaze travelled straight on, to the groups drinking outside the bar, to the starlet and the beauty queen, to a man in a beach-robe coming up the steps from the sea. She took them all in; she assessed them; and the result seemed to afford her a moderate satisfaction. Then she returned down the steps and entered the hotel.

'I have been affronted,' thought Janet Brocard.

It was some moments before she could see her resentment as absurd; but indeed she was not used to being looked at, or not looked at, as though she was without any distinct existence. Nor had the incident been imaginary, for even her two companions, as a rule so little open to social impressions, were turning to each other faces of mild surprise.

'I wonder what that girl was looking for?' said Professor Brocard.

3

THEY were to know soon enough. In the meantime, however, Janet, changing her dress, and receiving her husband's compliments, recovered her usual good temper; Harbin and Brocard

173

as usual donned their antique dinner-jackets, subsequently to condole with each other over this hard necessity; and they were settled as usual at the table farthest from the band, but with a good view of the room. All around them bottles of champagne protruded from buckets of ice, claret lay cradled in wicker, cocktails came on trays; but though the Brocards' table was supplied with nothing but water, it received very pleasant service. The hotel had a golfing tradition, which the presence of Harbin and the Professor (almost legendary figures of the course) reaffirmed; Janet's distinction was unmistakable; and moreover the cheques received at the end of their visit, though comparatively small, were never dud.

'The manager's a very decent chap,' announced Charles Harbin. 'I've just met him in the hall, and he asked me to tell Janet that if she cares to use the little sitting-room upstairs, he'll be very glad.'

'But that's private!' protested Janet.

'He said it hadn't been taken and he likes to have it used.'

'On a wet day, you'd find it very convenient,' advised the Professor. 'I call it extremely civil.'

'The thing is, Janet reminds him of his better days,' pronounced Harbin seriously. It was common knowledge that the manager had been brought to the Fort Flag from an old and famous but decaying London hotel; and though few persons would have considered this a come-down, Harbin's remark showed perception. 'She reminds him,' said Harbin, 'of pre-war . . .'

It was very pleasant to be together at the Fort Flag again. The three had a great deal in common, and because the Brocards saw Harbin only once a year, kept their friendship undulled by use. They had a great deal to talk about: Brocard's university was in the North, Harbin worked in London: they knew each other's lives by hearsay, and each other's colleagues like characters in a serial. The meal was nearly finished before there was any pause in the conversation; only over the ice did they fall into an easy silence, just as pleasant in its way, and just as familiar, as their easy talk.

Pleasant, easy and familiar, it was also brief. A fresh topic of conversation – which was also to be the main topic of their stay – even then approached across the hall. A waiter held the door: coolly, taking her time, moving gracefully between the crowded tables, the newest arrival entered the dining-room.

It was at once apparent that she had at least two good reasons for being so late. In the first place, her toilette represented a full hour's hard work, and in the second, it would have been wasted on any but a full house.

Her dress, of paper-white chiffon, was strapless, almost bodiless: a minimum of drapery curved in two small shells over the bosom, above a long, full, elaborately pleated skirt. The girl's very black, very silky hair, dressed in one high smooth roll, carried over each ear a big magnolia-flower, apparently of mother-of-pearl; and one arm, from wrist almost to elbow, was ringed with bangles only brighter, not more golden than her skin. Thus she was all white and gold and black, save for the bow of crimson lipstick painted on her mouth; for her eyes, when she raised them to the waiter, showed almost as dark as her hair.

'Dear me,' said Professor Brocard.

Janet looked at him affectionately. Every man in the room had contributed as it were his silent whistle: doubtless there were spoken – and out-spoken – comments as well: but not one, Janet felt sure, so endearingly inadequate.

'Is that the girl we saw get out of the wagon?' asked Harbin.

'Yes,' said Janet. 'I noticed her particularly.'

'Well, she's certainly very striking,' said Harbin. 'But – do you think she looks quite right?'

Janet hesitated. She was very generous: the girl made an undeniably beautiful show, and one would not have thought it possible, in the dining-room of the Fort Flag, on a Saturday night, for a woman to appear over-dressed. The beauty queen had put on gold lamé, the starlet twinkled from about fifty yards of shaded tulle; many of the other women were jewelled to the limit of their husband's credit. But none of these – and therein lay the difference – was alone. The girl should have had an escort. When she raised those dark eyes it should have been not to a waiter, but to a protector. No woman, thought Janet, because though the code is old it is still valid, should appear so in public, unprotected . . .

She became aware that Charles Harbin still waited enquiringly. A simple man, and a bachelor, he had for many years looked to Janet for all worldly wisdom.

'I think,' said Janet, 'it's because she's by herself.'

Charles Harbin considered this carefully.

'Perhaps,' he suggested at length, 'later on, she'll make a friend.'

'Perhaps she will,' agreed Janet – and at once saw the answer to the question her husband had asked on the terrace. For of course, that was what the girl was looking for: in the current idiom, a friend, in fact, a protector. 'And why not?' Janet asked herself.

'I call it bold,' said Professor Brocard. 'Even brazen. And yet –'

'And yet?' prompted Janet. Every now and again, when he could turn his attention from the geological to the human species, her husband surprised her by his shrewdness. It remained, in its impartiality, a little scientific; it was still surprising.

'If she hopes to make a conquest,' said the Professor, 'for you see I go further than Charles – and I can't help being reminded of the mating-plumage of certain birds – though *that*, of course, usually appertains to the male – if she *does* hope to make a conquest, is not so frank a display perhaps justified?'

'Do you mean justified or expedient?' asked Harbin.

'Both,' said the Professor promptly. 'What might or might not be justified is the original impulse. But if you take a young woman without family – would you say she was without family, Janet?'

'Without family to the purpose,' agreed Janet – uncontrollably vizualizing a father who dealt in hardware, a mother patient and perplexed, a younger sister at a commercial school.

'Very well, then. A young woman without family to back her pretensions, and those pretensions, by the accident of her beauty justifiably – (justifiably, Charles!) – high – unless she has an uncommon allowance of brains as well – surely against all the laws of averages – what course can she take but that of conquest? Would *you* say she had brains, Janet?'

'No,' said Janet. 'Or not what you call brains. But she is undoubtedly, within limits, clever.'

'Then there you are. Beauty, acuteness, probably no education. Appetites, of course. And possibly a limited time in which to turn the beauty to enough account to gratify the appetites. I dare say this is the great campaigning season of her life. So she has to make haste,' continued the Professor, 'she has to polish her bow and spear, and put them to immediate use. Hence the flower in the hair, the frank display of bosom, and the general – though indeed I now regret the word – brazenness.'

'You have certainly made a good case for her,' said Janet.

'I hope I have an open mind. But what we must next discover,' concluded the Professor briskly, and turning his chair the better to survey the room, 'is whether there is any suitable quarry. Which, Janet, are the most desirable males?'

With an unusual lack of detail Janet indicated a Tommy, a Bobby and a Peter, (the Fort Flag always attracted more unattached men than most hotels), a golfer or two and a sporting Belgian. The Professor surveyed them carefully, as he might have surveyed a class of honours students, and observed that they offered a pretty fair field.

'Though of course one must allow for wastage,' he pointed out. 'Some of them may be leaving. On the other hand, there may be more to come. Janet, my dear, we look to you for news of the campaign.'

'I'm not sure I shall follow it,' said Janet. 'I'm not sure it will amuse me.'

4

BUT she could not help following it. When the heroine of a musical comedy has made her entrance, a concerted number inevitably follows, and amid the swelling chorus of information and theory, comment and speculation, Janet Brocard for the first time felt her solitude vulnerable. No longer, when she sat sewing on the terrace, did fellow-guests praise her embroidery and pass on. They praised and stayed. Or at least the women did. The men were mostly concentrated elsewhere – on the beach, if Miss Duval was bathing, or on the tennis-court, if Miss Duval was playing tennis, or, if Miss Duval was thirsty, in the bar.

'Don't you think it's a vewwy odd name?' lisped the beauty

queen, standing meekly by Janet's chair. 'I mean, Tanya Duval — that's what she *says* it is — well, it doesn't seem to *match*, does it? I mean, one's Wussian, and the other's Fwench.'

'Perhaps she had bilingual parents,' suggested Janet rather unkindly. The beauty queen examined the adjective for a moment, and abandoned it.

'Well, *I* think it sounds made up,' she persisted.

So did Janet. She also thought it none of their business; but added (the impulse to educate always strong in her) that any one, by deed poll, could take any name they liked. The beauty queen looked shocked.

'I don't think that's vewwy nice,' she said firmly. 'I mean, my name's Smike, and when I won the pwize I could see they were disappointed: but I wouldn't have changed it, not for ever so.'

She pattered off, righteous but a little disconsolate: Janet did not know whether to be glad or sorry that Miss Smike's holiday was proving a disappointment. On the whole, she thought, glad: at least the child would not have her head turned — for the fact was that with all her prettiness Miss Smike's conversation was so flat, and her virtue so impregnable, that the Fort Flag found her a dreadful little bore. The Beauty Editress in particular was bored, for chaperonage works both ways, and she had learnt to detest Miss Smike's reproving eye.

'I'm an adult woman, my dear,' she complained to Janet. 'I know quite well there's poison in the grape, I've been absorbing it in moderate quantities for years, and it agrees with me. Miss Smike's a teetotaller, of course — that's one reason she got the prize. Personally I prefer La Tanya.'

As this was the first good word any one had spoken for Miss Duval, Janet waited with some interest.

'I'd trust her no more than a snake, of course,' added the

Editress cheerfully, 'but at least she wouldn't nestle in my bosom. She says she's a dress-designer: I know dam' well she's not: she's a model. I saw her myself at one of the Spring shows.'

'Models must be very well paid,' said Janet.

'Not well enough to vacation at the Fort Flag, my dear – though her clothes won't have cost so very much. However, as I hear our Belgian friend has already invited her to Brussels, at least she'll make expenses. Though in my opinion,' summed up this expert, 'she's after something more solid.'

The starlet could afford to be detached. Her band-leader was a fixture; they had been photographed together daily, the hints of their romance were already released, and they weren't going to waste the publicity.

'*I* think she's extremely pretty – don't you, Mrs Brocard?' purred the starlet. 'I think people are being very unkind about her. Of course if *I* behaved like that my studio would be *furious*; but then I've a five-year contract – besides darling Nick,' threw in the starlet conscientiously – 'and *my* future's in the bag. But I think if a girl's as pretty as that, and perhaps has a little money saved up, she's quite right to give herself a taste of gaiety. It will always be something to remember – don't you think so, Mrs Brocard?'

'You mean when she's scrubbing floors?' suggested Janet.

'That's just what I do mean. And *I* think other people are so unkind not to see it. *I* only hope that all her memories will be *happy* . . .'

Mrs Robins was much franker. Mrs Robins was one of the stout under-clad matrons, whom Janet suspected of being a secret knitter. She had admired Janet's embroidery, frankly and loudly, from the first day, and so approached with the confidence of an old friend.

'*I* think it's scandalous,' proclaimed Mrs Robins. 'And it's not on account of my girls – *they* didn't come here to catch husbands, they can have the pick of the basket at home. I just think it's scandalous, the dead set she's making at that poor young man.'

Janet glanced along the terrace – following the angry eye of Mrs Robins – to the poor young man in question. He was the one called Tommy. He wasn't really poor, of course: he exhibited, in his car and his clothes and his drinking habits, all the signs of wealth; but as he now followed Miss Duval up the steps from the sea – thin as a skinned rabbit, dripping like a ducked pup, laden with rubber beach-toys – he looked at once so meagre and so foolish as amply to justify Mrs Robins' description. Moreover, he was quite obviously infatuated; when Tanya turned and spoke to him, he looked up with a wide idiotic grin; she had to speak twice before he understood that the toys should have been left below.

In the next moment Janet was suddenly touched to the heart.

She did not wish to be touched; she kept her heart rather carefully; but poor Tommy got under her guard. For he simply let the toys drop – the paddle, the quoit, the big rubber horse – so that they flopped down the steps behind him, to the sand below. Because Tanya did not want them, they no longer existed . . .

'I believe I shall go in,' said Janet. 'The sun's a little too much for me.'

Though the weather was remarkably good, Janet was indeed finding the small upstairs sitting-room a great convenience. She was not, however, to enjoy it long, for after two or three days the manager apologetically informed her that it had been taken, as part of a suite booked by a gentleman arriving at mid-week. Janet had to conceal a genuine regret: her husband, on the other hand, who had so warmly recommended its acceptance, was rather pleased. He suspected that Janet had spent too much time there, to the neglect of her duties as special correspondent: if he and Harbin hadn't used their own eyes, complained the Professor, they might never have known about the nobbling of Poor Tommy.

'For nobbled he is,' diagnosed Professor Brocard, as they sat down to dinner on the Wednesday night. 'Nobbled, lassoed, or, if you will, hooked.'

'Harpooned,' suggested Charles Harbin.

'Too final,' objected the Professor.

'Not in these days. They shoot the harpoon from a sort of gun, I believe at quite long range. The whale has still to be brought in.'

'Then I accept the harpoon. Tommy has been nobbled, lassoed, hooked, harpooned – and all in four days' flat. Dinner-time Saturday to dinner-time Wednesday. I call it remarkable.'

'Hotels are like liners,' said Janet. 'All emotions are forced.'

'I still say it's a remarkable performance. You observe, of course, that Tommy has changed his place?'

Janet had observed it at lunch-time. Poor Tommy and Miss Duval were not yet at the same table, but they had tables side by side, with an ice-bucket permanently between them. Such re-arrangements were by no means unusual at the Fort Flag, but this one had caused more than the usual amount of talk; Janet inclined to agree with the magnanimous starlet that people were very unkind about Miss Duval. 'Perhaps she genuinely likes Poor Tommy,' thought Janet. 'After all, why shouldn't she? They're very much of a kind; they're much of an age, they appear to share the same deplorable tastes; she may even think him good-looking.'

'He isn't actually repulsive,' said Janet aloud.

'He repels *me*,' retorted the Professor instantly.

'He's no worse-looking than some of your students. He's only weedy. His features are really quite good.'

'Their expression defines vacuity,' said the Professor. 'My students, indeed! – there's not an idle little runt amongst them wouldn't make ten of your Poor Tommy.'

The general verdict of the hotel, though not quite so harsh, agreed with Professor Brocard. Miss Duval had nobbled Poor Tommy, and from mercenary motives alone: it only remained to be seen whether she could clinch the matter with an engagement-ring, or even a special licence, while his infatuation still lasted. – For on another point also opinion was solid: Miss Duval's objective. She was no good-time girl. (She wanted no no trips to Brussels, thank you very much.) Her intentions were strictly honorable.

The situation was still in this highly interesting juncture when there arrived at the Fort Flag a chauffeur-driven Rolls. It arrived, in fact, the next morning; and out of it stepped a small, grey-haired, elderly man in a very tidy tweed suit, whom the manager was there to greet in person; for this was Mr Cook, who had engaged the first-floor suite, and with it Janet's lost sitting-room.

5

ANY new arrival, particularly at mid-week, was certain to attract attention: Mr Cook attracted it particularly, and paradoxically, by behaviour which anywhere else would have been inconspicuous to vanishing-point. He never, for example, sun-bathed, but always went fully clad, except when actually in the sea. His sports clothes, though all new, were all conservative: white flannels and tweed jackets, a neat blue bathing-dress and a towelling beach-robe rather too large for him: he had some nice blue shirts, open at the neck, and one of timid plaid. His only noticeable possession was a panama hat whose superlative quality was as obvious as a price-ticket: this he wore constantly when out of doors, and doffed politely (though mutely) when passing a lady. In short, he cut such a figure as would have made him the joke of the hotel, if he hadn't been a millionaire.

'But there are no millionaires nowadays!' objected Janet. 'They've all been taxed away!'

'Plumbers are always in demand,' said the Professor. 'Our friend the manager informs me that this is none other than A. D. Cook, maker and layer of sewers. I have no doubt he is very comfortably off.'

In general, however, Mr Cook was spoken of as a contractor; every one wished to be civil to him. But this was not easy: Mr Cook, either from diffidence or pride kept very much to himself. He used his sitting-room a great deal, and the bars not at all; and as things turned out the first person he made friends with was Janet Brocard.

She had left, in that sitting-room, and never missed, a half-skein of crimson wool. An indifferent house-maid thrust it into the blotter; a couple of days after his arrival Mr Cook found it; and by careful observation – Janet had noticed him once or twice looking narrowly at her embroidery – decided to whom it belonged. Panama hat in one hand, the wool in the other, he firmly approached; and the very firmness of his step told Janet that he wasn't a proud man, but a shy.

'That's very nice of you,' she said. 'It belongs – see? – to my rose.'

'I guessed it did,' said Mr Cook. He looked pleased, but still diffident. 'If,' he said, 'you used that room yourself, ever, I'm sorry to have turned you out.'

'But it was never mine!' protested Janet.

'I don't like to be doing it,' persisted Mr Cook.

He was so obviously sincere, and so obviously troubled, that Janet impulsively moved her work-bag from the next chair and invited him to sit down.

So began what the rest of the hotel rather maliciously (and enviously) referred to as their beautiful friendship. Janet did not mind this joke in the least: she liked Mr Cook, and if he chose to spend most of the day at her side rather welcomed his company. In the evenings he was shyer, for he had the old-fashioned respect for academic learning, and though the Professor and Charles Harbin liked him very well, Janet suspected Mr Cook of finding their conversation erratic. Mr Cook, the millionaire, had so to speak no conversation at all: with all his practical ability, any rapid give and take of ideas was quite beyond him. What Mr Cook liked was to sit comfortably beside a nice woman and talk about himself.

As for Janet, who had never met anyone of his type before, she was constantly astounded by its contradictions. In everything that pertained to his work Mr Cook was so obviously hard-headed, experienced, resourceful and open-minded: if the Caliph of Baghdad dropped in about a new sewerage system, thought Janet, Mr Cook wouldn't turn a hair; but in most other directions he was simply ignorant, and in his private character quite extraordinarily unsophisticated. The possession of wealth seemed to have left no mark on him whatever; if he had a big house, he bought it (he told Janet) because it was a bargain, and near his works; and if he had a Rolls-Royce it was because he needed some sort of car, and a good one saved trouble.

'So was my bicycle a good 'un,' said Mr Cook, with a faint smile. 'Mother saw to that.'

Janet heard a lot about Mr Cook's mother: how, in the years when he went straight to night-school after a day's work, she always sat up for him with a little snack of something hot: how she put her own savings to his to buy the bicycle, so that he could get out into the country on Sundays: how when he brought her back a bunch of flowers she always made a great fuss of them, and arranged them in a big pot in the front window. 'I made her very comfortable before she died,' said Mr Cook. 'I like to think of it.' Janet heard also about his wife, a gentle little thing, very loving, for whom motherhood had proved too hard an ordeal; and how when she left him he put everything but work out of his mind, and in a worldly sense prospered greatly. 'You may not credit it,' said Mr Cook, 'but this is the first holiday I've taken in twenty years. So I reckoned I'd have a good 'un.'

'And how are you enjoying it?' asked Janet. 'What do you think of the Fort Flag?'

'It's a bit much for me,' said Mr Cook.

The truth was that he was shocked. He was shocked by the sun-bathing and the drinking and the spending: he was shocked by the open flirtations and by the dancing cheek-to-cheek. But he was trying not to let on, because his suite was costing him twenty guineas a day, without board.

'I'll stick it out another week,' said Mr Cook.

Had Janet been gifted with prophecy she would have taken hold of him then and there, and hustled him up to his rooms, and stood over him while he packed; she wouldn't have let Mr Cook out of her sight until he was safely in his Rolls, headed for home.

6

On the second Thursday of the Brocards' stay, exactly a week after the arrival of Mr Cook, Janet had just settled in her usual place on the terrace when she saw a girl she did not know come out of the hotel. The illusion lasted but a moment; for that moment, it had been complete. Even after Janet recognized her, Tanya Duval, in a white short-sleeved dress, her hair smoothed back under a round comb, wearing practically no make-up, still looked a good deal more like Alice in Wonderland than like Tanya Duval.

No one else was about; indeed breakfast, for the majority of the guests, had hardly been thought of. Miss Duval approached Janet's chair and halted.

'How beautifully you embroider!' said Miss Duval.

'Thank you,' said Janet. Her voice was as cold as her eye; she could as a rule very easily rid herself of unwelcome attentions. But Miss Duval sat down on the terrace and clasped her arms round her knees.

'I wish *I* could embroider like that. But of course you have to have wonderful taste.'

Janet said nothing. After a few moments Miss Duval pushed a slim finger (with unvarnished nail) into the big work-bag.

'Shall I sort your wools for you?'

'Thank you,' said Janet again, 'no.'

'But I'd like to,' said Miss Duval – and had the wools in her lap before you could say knife.

Janet looked down at the black head, at the slim neck bent so earnestly over a child's pretty task, and felt extremely annoyed, but there was nothing to be done short of getting up and walking away, and she did not choose to disturb herself. No doubt Poor Tommy would soon appear to disburden her; for it was at Poor Tommy, Janet suspected, that this sudden maidenliness was really aimed. Perhaps he had shown himself too much of a thruster; perhaps Tanya needed to complete her campaign from behind conventional defences . . .

The person who first appeared, however, was not Poor Tommy but Mr Cook. Janet, bent on her work, did not see him come; if Tanya saw, she kept silence.

'May I spoil the picture?' asked Mr Cook.

Janet glanced sharply up. Mr Cook was looking at Tanya. He had seen her already, of course, continually; but not in a white schoolgirl dress, not with her hair sleeked back under a round comb.

'Of course,' said Janet automatically. 'Here's your chair.'

Mr Cook sat. It was evident that he felt both surprise and pleasure; he caught Janet's eye with an approving smile. Tanya, peeping shyly up under her lashes, managed to catch his eye as well.

'Are you an embroideress too?' asked Mr Cook.

'Oh, no,' murmured Tanya. 'I'm just sorting Mrs Brocard's wools for her.'

Janet repressed an impulse to smack the chit and went on with her work. Tanya went on sorting, and Mr Cook went on looking at Tanya. All three presented a fallacious picture of companionable silence. There were few to observe it, however; the terrace was still almost empty; and in fact as the first of the other guests began to appear, Tanya jumped to her feet with a little sound of dismay.

'How dreadful of me!' she cried. 'I've just remembered – to-morrow's a birthday! I must run all the way to the shops and buy a present. And – oh, dear – it's so hot!'

Eagerly Mr Cook rose to the simple bait.

'Won't you let me take you,' he offered, 'in my car?'

'*Oh!*' gasped Tanya, quite overcome. 'In your beautiful Rolls? I've never *been* in a Rolls! Mrs Brocard, won't you come too?'

Mrs Brocard, however, would not. During the rest of the day (the Rolls failing to return until nearly six) annoyance and uneasiness so gained on her, and the gossip caused by Tanya's exploit became so intolerable, that she went up and sat in her bedroom until her husband came home.

'What's the matter?' asked Professor Brocard. 'Is anything wrong?'

'Yes,' said Janet. 'I've been used as a stalking-horse; and I don't like it.'

7

MR COOK'S view of the situation, however, which he made haste to lay before Janet that same evening, was quite different. Mr Cook was delighted. He and Miss Duval had had a splendid day together – first shopping, then lunch, then a walk over the cliffs – but no part of it had given him more pleasure than Tanya's frequent references to Mrs Brocard. For if Mr Cook admired Janet, so did Tanya; if Mr Cook considered Janet distinguished, sensible and kind, Tanya considered her beautiful, brilliant and gracious. This made such a bond between them that Mr Cook (himself bound to Janet already) confidently vizualized a triple knot of friendship including all three.

Tanya was certainly a fast worker, and she had had a good innings – nearly eight hours tête-à-tête. Even so, Janet was astonished at the completeness of the picture Mr Cook could now reflect: there were not even any questions to ask, they had all been answered in advance. For instance –

'Right from the start it was you she wanted to make friends with,' explained Mr Cook earnestly. 'Only she was too shy. That's how she came to get in with all the riff-raff – they made a fuss of her while she was lonely. She was wondering all the time what you'd think of her. She says as soon as she saw you, you reminded her of her mother.'

('This is too much!' thought Janet furiously. 'I won't stand it! I will not remind La Tanya of her mum!')

'I was very forthright with her,' continued the oblivious Mr Cook. 'I told her straight out *my* first impression of her had been that she was . . . fast. So then she told me a lot more – how she hadn't really been drinking at all, only ginger-ale, because it looked like whisky – and when I asked her why she wanted to be taken for a whisky-drinker, what do you think she said?'

'I've no idea,' said Janet. 'But I should like to hear.'

'She said those oafs would laugh if they knew she was teetotal! It fairly made my blood boil. "*I*'ll drink lemonade with you, any time you like," I said, "and if anyone laughs at *me* I shall be very much surprised." I made her promise never to go into the bar without me. And then, I told her, there's your make-up.'

'Wasn't that rather bold of you?'

'She was – well, she was fairly opening her heart to me. She *asked* me, poor child, after I'd said she looked fast, to pretend . . . well, to pretend for a minute she was my daughter. Did I tell you she was an orphan?'

'As a matter of fact, I'd guessed it,' said Janet. 'I presumed her mother, whom I am said to resemble, is no more.'

'That's right. There's just little Tanya, and a baby brother.

He's who the present was for. They both live with their Grannie.'

Janet found it necessary to remind herself that all this information had issued from an uncommonly pretty mouth (only faintly pink) and had been corroborated, no doubt, by many a melting glance from a pair of soft, dark, un-mascara'd eyes. She had every respect for Tanya's power to bamboozle a middle-aged, innocent male. But she herself was not bamboozled; and now, suddenly, she did not want to hear even why Tanya used to put on too much make-up. She could no longer see the girl, as the Professor did, as an interesting human specimen, or sport; she found Tanya too dangerous to be amusing; and rather abruptly excusing herself from further conversation, left Mr Cook to his happy thoughts.

'After all,' thought Janet wishfully, 'he's only here till Saturday week. Even Tanya can't do much damage in ten days.'

8

BUT an hotel, as she herself had pointed out, is as much a forcing-house of the emotions as any ocean-liner; within not ten days, but two, Tanya and Mr Cook were on terms of such intimacy that Janet's company (which they both continued to seek) afforded merely chaperonage. She was no longer a stalking-horse, but a gooseberry. It was a situation both painful and ludicrous, and Janet could only hope that the rest of her fellow-guests were less keenly alive to it than she was herself.

In point of fact, every one else at the Fort Flag, whether they reprobated Tanya or applauded her, whether they wished her luck or held up their hands, found the affair essentially stimulating. It gave them something to talk about, focused their interest; it was an incident, a drama, almost a sporting event. The only exception was Poor Tommy. Poor Tommy had taken Tanya's change of aim hard, and was indeed drinking steadily, from noon till midnight, conventionally drowning his sorrows.

Poor Tommy was deplorable. Everyone sympathized with his despair, but he attracted rescue-parties only to repel them. The barmen did their best for him with ice-water in his martinis – a kindly ruse that largely failed of its effect owing to the weakness of Poor Tommy's head. But on the whole this disability proved an advantage: his wits packed up on him in the first stages of melancholia, and he harmlessly slept out his sorrows either in public or on his bed.

Tanya told Mr Cook that if there was one thing she hated, it was to see anyone under the influence of alcohol.

Tanya's own behaviour, at any rate towards her new admirer, was, quite literally, enchanting. She had Mr Cook spellbound. Shy and modest as a violet, she did not exactly discourage his attentions, but received them with an air of diffident surprise. She was a girl, Janet noted, almost with admiration, who could commandeer a Rolls *timidly*. She accepted all his gifts – timidly. So far, indeed, Mr Cook had given her nothing but flowers and lemonade, and the flowers were always inexpensive, for Tanya quite hated orchids; but what might he not give her, once he had the right? 'Why settle for orchids, when you can get diamonds?' thought Janet – and was dismayed by her own vulgarity.

The Professor, when at last she voiced her distress to him, was genuinely astonished.

'But what are you worrying about?' he enquired. 'Why shouldn't Cook be nobbled like anyone else?'

'Because he's too simple,' said Janet. 'Too — innocent. I think he's fallen in love with her.'

'Just what I say. He's nobbled.'

'Suppose he asks her to marry him?'

'Then the chase will have been even more successful than one had hoped,' replied Professor Brocard, 'and I trust we shall be in at the death.' He looked at his wife sharply. 'I hope you don't think of doing anything about it?'

'I only wish I could,' said Janet. 'Why not?'

'It would be upsetting the balance of nature. As soon as man takes sides against any predatory animal, such as the fox, he finds himself over-run by its natural prey, such as the rabbit. Look what happened in Australia.'

'But rabbits were introduced into Australia.'

'Exactly – by man. It all comes,' said the Professor rather hastily, 'to the same thing. And as millionaires are the natural prey of gold-diggers, let Cook take his chance.'

If Janet did so, it was because she saw no alternative. What argument, after all, could she produce in Tanya's disfavour? To say baldly, 'That brat ignored me until I became your friend, and then used me as a stalking-horse,' would find Mr Cook only too ready with an answer: that Tanya had *not* been ignoring Mrs Brocard, on the contrary: she had been worshipping from afar; and there was moreover something extremely disagreeable in such tale-bearing. Janet therefore did nothing; and with a week of holiday still to run found herself eagerly looking forward to the day when she could go home. If her husband wanted to be in at the death, she did not; if the drama were approaching a climax, she did not wish to see it.

For a day or two longer, however, the dénouement hung fire. Mr Cook had not quite lost his head – and indeed, in a peculiar way, showed no sign of doing so. 'Innocent,' Janet had called him: and it was as though the idea of making love to Tanya had never entered his head. 'But she's only to fall into his arms,' thought Janet – and meant it literally. Tanya needed only to break the last barrier with a physical contact, and Mr Cook was done for. She needed only to fall into his arms.

On the following Wednesday evening, Tanya did so.

9

It was an evening marked, as every now and then an evening at the Fort Flag was so marked, by a burst of unsophisticated merriment. It began in the ball-room, where a double conga-line suddenly translated itself into the game of Oranges and Lemons; presently the ball-room was empty, because all the younger guests, and a good many old enough to know better, were out on the terrace playing hide-and-seek. A moon rose over the darkening sea; the seekers began to seek in couples, the hiders were harder and harder to find; in the laughter and the running to and fro there was something childish and yet not childish, an abandon which childishness only just masked. The Professor and Charles Harbin, noting only an unusual degree of rowdiness, retired upstairs to play chess, but Janet, on so beautiful a night, could not bear to be within doors, and walked along the terrace to its farther end, where the steps came up from the beach, and where the open, balustraded space afforded too little cover to attract the games-party. That part of the terrace was quite empty, and so were the moon-washed sands below, for the evening was yet too young for the mid-night-bathing frolic in which it was certainly going to end. 'Let me enjoy the night, while I may,' thought Janet – and in the same moment realized that she was not so entirely solitary as she had believed. The sands below were not quite empty, after all: across the bright path of the moon moved the small, dark figure of Mr Cook.

He was pacing slowly back and forth along the rim of the tide: neat, composed, and utterly out of place. He wasn't made for a romantic background. Night and the boundless sea, in conjunction with A. D. Cook, suggested merely the danger of catching cold. If he felt himself too old, and too sober, for the fun-and-games above, he was of course perfectly right; but he was also too old to pace damp sand in thin shoes. Janet leant over the balustrade, meaning to call out and warn him; then the thought that he might be waiting there for Tanya, that they had a rendezvous there on the shore, momentarily held her back. She hesitated: if it *was* a rendezvous, might she not be doing very well to prevent it? Might it not be the saving, in fact, of Mr Cook, to turn a tête-à-tête into a trio? Janet looked, leaned down again, and hesitated – and hesitated a moment too long.

There was a sound of flying feet behind her. Tanya, running like a deer, shadowy as a white moth, came skimming over the terrace flagstones before an unseen pursuer. She ran straight to the steps, and almost threw herself down them; and missed her footing, and cried out, and landed sobbing and breathless, but safe, in Mr Cook's arms.

Janet never saw who the pursuer was. He halted, and turned rather sheepishly aside, as she passed him on her way back indoors. She saw nothing more at all: but when, on the following morning, as she was going down to breakfast, Mr Cook waylaid her outside the door of his sitting-room, and asked whether she had a few minutes to spare, Janet had no doubt in the world of what he was going to tell her.

10

As she followed him into the room she saw that he was again wearing his tweed suit: beside the desk stood a strapped suit-case, on the sofa lay a strapped brief-case, a mackintosh and a light overcoat. Mr Cook followed her glance, and nodded.

'That's right,' he said. 'I'm leaving.'

'But – today?' exclaimed Janet – and even as she spoke saw the reason: Tanya at least might well find the congratulations of the Fort Flag embarrassingly hearty . . .

'That's right,' repeated Mr Cook. 'In about ten minutes. I just wanted to tell you. If you don't mind, I'll light a pipe.'

He did so, very carefully; halfway through the operation observed with dismay that Janet was still on her feet, and paused to push the coats off the sofa. She sat down and waited; it was a moment like the moment before one opens a telegram containing certain ill news. 'This one,' thought Janet, 'will say that Tanya too has her luggage packed, and is waiting in the Rolls . . .'

'There's no fool like an old fool,' said Mr Cook suddenly. 'Is there?'

'But *you* aren't a fool!' said Janet – her voice sounding light and formal, but not, she hoped, insincere.

'Then it's been a near shave,' said Mr Cook. '*You*'ve seen how things are with me. You've seen me lose my heart to little Tanya. And now it's come to the point where I've got to clear out, because if I don't I shall be asking her to marry me. But I couldn't go without a word to you first.'

Janet, who found that for the last few seconds she had actually been holding her breath, sighed an absurd relief. For it *was* absurd, she told herself – reacting almost with impatience, almost with anger – to have become so involved in Mr Cook's affairs, and absurd not to have perceived his essential hard-headedness – and absurd to feel, now, that she could almost kiss him for his good sense. At the same time, she did not wish to appear too congratulatory: Mr Cook was still looking no more than resigned.

'I think you're quite right,' she said. 'I think you're very sensible.'

'She's too good for me,' said Mr Cook.

Janet's mind as a rule worked very quickly: now, for a moment, it seemed to stop working altogether, it simply contemplated with astonishment the mind of Mr Cook. What an image of Tanya was therein reflected! – 'And yet I have seen it all along,' thought Janet, re-mustering her wits. 'I knew how he idealized her. But I under-estimated his magnanimity, I mistook it for shrewdness, and it is my own fault that now I don't know how to help him . . .'

'*You* know little Tanya,' Mr Cook was saying. 'You're the only one here she took to. A lovely child . . . I'm fifty-four, I go to the works in the morning and come home from the works at night, and take a look at the papers, and maybe play a game of cards with another old codger like myself. What sort of a life would that be for her?'

This time he waited for an answer; and impulsively, against her better judgment, Janet reminded him of an asset he seemed to forget.

'Well, after all,' she pointed out, 'you're a very rich man.'

Once again Mr Cook surprised her.

'Aye,' he said, 'there's that. Tanya might marry me for my money. But what sort of a chap should I be, to put such a temptation in her way?'

11

So Mr Cook escaped. He left the hotel immediately; Janet was the only person he said good-bye to, and by the time Tanya came down to breakfast the Rolls was already some dozen miles on its homeward route. But there was a note under Miss Duval's plate, and Janet, seeing her about to open it, rather hastily left the dining-room and made her way again to the terrace-end. Janet was experiencing an extreme lightness of spirit, she rejoiced from her heart at such a signal triumph of innocence as she could still hardly grasp; but at the same time realized that Tanya was unlikely to take defeat quietly. Tanya would be spoiling for a row, and most probably for a row with her admired Mrs Brocard; and Janet, though very willing to get it over as soon as possible, preferred a more secluded terrain than the dining-room. Sure enough, within five minutes, Tanya was at her side, – a Tanya white with anger, a Tanya incoherent with bewilderment, a Tanya whose furious hands had twisted and torn at Mr Cook's letter until it was scarcely legible even when thrust under Janet's nose. Janet made it out, however: a brief statement of unexpected business calls, a brief line of good wishes, and the brief, formal signature, *Sincerely A. D. Cook*. That was all: either Mr Cook did not know how to express himself more romantically, or else he had determined to show romance an altogether clean pair of heels.

'Yes,' said Janet, 'I know. I saw him this morning.'

'I thought so. What lies did you tell him about me?'

The insult, though not unexpected, forced Janet to pause and control herself before answering.

'I told him nothing,' she said. 'All he knows of you he found out for himself.'

Tanya took a menacing step nearer.

'But he was crazy about me! Last night, he was crazy about me!'

'And this morning he has gone home,' said Janet. She had no intention of explaining Mr Cook's motive: Tanya could scarcely be expected to appreciate it, all that would lodge in her head was the notion that he was crazy still – perhaps crazy enough to be worth pursuing. 'You over-did it,' said Janet bluntly. 'You over-did it, with your girlish ways. You made him feel old enough to be your grandfather.'

'But I didn't care how old he was! I'll never get such a chance again! I'd have married him if he'd been ninety!'

'Exactly,' retorted Janet. 'So Mr Cook probably realized.'

With the first genuinely childish gesture Janet had ever seen in her, Tanya jerked away and kicked angrily at the stone of the balustrade. The impact must have been painful, for she was wearing only sandals: but she kicked out again, hurting herself as a child in a tantrum hurts itself, partly out of sheer rage – and partly, Janet remembered, in order to attract adult consolation. And in spite of herself, Janet consoled.

'Of course you'll have other chances,' she said. 'What about Poor Tommy?'

Tanya stopped kicking and began to cry.

'Tommy's no use. He hasn't anything really. He came into a bit of money and he's just blueing it.'

'He was extremely devoted to you,' said Janet.

'Well, I liked *him*,' muttered Tanya. 'We were having a good time together. I liked him much better than Mr Cook. If you want to know, we . . . we were properly gone on each other. It's not nearly so easy being hard-boiled as you seem to think.' Tanya sniffed loudly. '*Now* he's drinking his head off . . .'

'You selfish little beast,' said Janet. 'Go and stop him.'

12

IT was the custom of the Fort Flag orchestra to play 'Happy Birthday to You' at least two or three times a week. Sometimes there was a genuine birthday to celebrate; sometimes the recipient of these musical honours had merely won a tennis tournament or a spot-dance; at all events it made for gaiety, and if the violinist's sense of humour now and then ran away with him – he played 'Happy Birthday' four times running for Mrs Robins' poodle's pups – it was really to his credit that he retained a sense of humour at all. When he played 'Happy Birthday' because Miss Duval and Poor Tommy were once more seated at adjacent tables, every one thought it a very good joke; and when he went on playing until, amid laughter and shifting of places, they actually moved opposite to each other, the whole dining-room broke into applause.

'Dear me,' said Professor Brocard. 'So it's Poor Tommy after all!'

'Yes,' said Janet. 'He's landed.'

'Poor Tommy indeed!'

'Poor Tommy and poor Tanya,' said Janet. 'They'll lead a raffish sort of life. But at least they're two of a kind.'

'Poor Cook,' said Charles Harbin suddenly. 'There was a time when I thought he'd lost his head.'

'He was a wise fellow, he cut and run,' said the Professor.

Janet said nothing. The thought of Mr Cook filled her

with a pleasure which she did not particularly want to submit to her husband's analysis. She even felt moderately happy about Tanya and Poor Tommy. All the same, she was very glad that on the following day she would be going home.